Beyond a Near Water

Beyond a Near Water

Book One

of

The Long Reflection

***

Patrick Jasper Lee

B
O
K
T
A
L
⊙

Published by Boktalo Book & Music Publishers

Boktalo Book & Music Publishers
PO Box 171
Hailsham
BN27 9AA

A catalogue record for this book is available from the British Library.

ISBN 0-9549695-0-2

Printed by Antony Rowe Ltd

To Lizzie and Martyn
who remember

Contents

Acknowledgements

I would like to thank all those who have made the first book in this series possible:

My many students and friends who have believed in this venture and who understand what this book has to offer, and particularly the small few who understand the real ancient world; James Alvis of Antony Rowe, for stepping in during a time of need; Steve, for being there at the right moment with his wonderful artistic skills; my copy editor, Lizzie H. for her tireless support, continuous encouragement and practical help; Puro, for his wisdom and insights, many of which went into this book; and Lizzie, my partner, for her belief in me and for her dedication to my work.

Chronology

* = the seventh of seven generations: the one who is chosen to step into the Long Reflection.

Book One: Beyond a Near Water
The Eleventh Hala
* Horki born 1055
  child of Horki
  grandchild of Horki
  great-grandchild of Horki
  great-great-grandchild of Horki
  great-great-great-grandchild of Horki
  great-great-great-great-grandchild of Horki

The Thirteenth Hala
* Ruslo Ruk born 1238
  child of Ruk
  grandchild of Ruk
  great-grandchild of Ruk
  great-great-grandchild of Ruk
  great-great-great-grandchild of Ruk
  great-great-great-great-grandchild of Ruk

Book Two: Through Forest Mist
The Fifteenth Hala
* Lenore and Lileskai born 1423
  child of Lenore

grandchild of Lenore
great-grandchild of Lenore
great-great-grandchild of Lenore
great-great-great-grandchild of Lenore
great-great-great-great-grandchild of Lenore

The Seventeenth Hala
* No Name born 1588
child of No Name
grandchild of No Name
great-grandchild of No Name
great-great-grandchild of No Name
great-great-great-grandchild of No Name
great-great-great-great-grandchild of No Name

Book Three: Around Dark Fires
The Nineteenth Hala
* Jukal born 1803
child of Jukal
grandchild of Jukal
great-grandchild of Jukal
great-great-grandchild of Jukal
great-great-great-grandchild of Jukal
great-great-great-great-grandchild of Jukal

The Twenty-first Hala
* Tikni Chirikli born 1960

(?)

Prehistory: The Indo-European world

Iuzio the Immortal's First Tale

I stand beside the river, watching my reflection dance. I think of what has been and what is to come. I think of the generations stretching ahead of me and stretching behind. The sky begins to darken.

Chi? Can you hear me? Can you hear me calling to you along the road of time? Can we look into the water now and see one another's reflections, I at the beginning of this long road and you at its end?

Of course we can't. Not yet. And there is the possibility that we may never do so.

And what knows itself through constantly seeing itself, Chi?

Can you answer this riddle?

If you should find and feel the answer within your soul, you will soon see me standing here beside you, simply, as I am. If you never find the answer, you may never know me, in the whole of your life, because you will not have found your soul.

And this sounds very serious, Chi, doesn't it? And, it is, of course. You must prepare yourself for riddles. For they will keep coming. They are a part of the old world and

1

you will hear many as you attempt to see yourself in the River of Life.

What reflects the trees, the sky, the dwellings, the people, the animals, the birds and the landscape? I will soon be asking. My hope is that you will ask and answer such riddles yourself.

Are things topsy-turvy and not at all as they appear to be? Isn't that what these riddles are saying to you?

Think, Chi, think. Where is the reflection? Is the reflection in the river? Or might it be that you yourself are the reflection?

Remember that life as you know it will inevitably turn everything upside down, inside out and on its head. And there is no doubt that you will need to see things in this topsy-turvy way if you wish to make sense of what I am saying.

Oh, there are so many things I need to say to you, Chi, at this difficult hour, so much, on this quiet evening. And you will, at first, not understand my language. But you are there so clearly when I return my eyes to the river. I see you, but you don't see me. I see your face just as I have always seen it, and your eyes briefly looking into mine, for just a fleeting second. You are not able to hold your gaze for very long. Soon you are looking past me, like a baby who is constantly trying to bring the world into focus.

No. You won't remember who I am, no matter how many times I speak your name. I have become un-noticeable, part of your backdrop, something that merges with leaves, with rain, with cars, with houses, with your teacup in the mornings. I have become a single droplet of water in a vast expanse of sea.

And all because you learned how to forget.

And that means I will be the only one who will be able to see you, at least for now, perhaps because I am the only one who remembers how it really used to be.

But I also realise with a sinking heart that the time is coming when everyone all over the world will forget. Yes, the sky darkens as I speak. The time is coming when memory will enter a great silence. And all people will lose their sight.

So will I be able to bring you and all my other children home to themselves? Will you, Chi, and Horki and Ruk and others who come after and who come before you, learn enough to see yourselves in the River of Life and help me complete my task?

Can I act out this difficult role and get away with what I have to do? Because I am going to have to work in a seemingly underhand way behind the scenes and many will not like what I am doing. But there is no doubt that I will be able to do very little at all unless I have everyone's help. And I need your help most, Chi. We have the most difficult task on our hands.

I will have to move with so many generations, like a bird skilfully riding the winds of a rough storm. And the winds may sometimes knock me off course and the driving rain may sometimes cause me to want to turn back. And I will need to move through aeons of time, through the many hundreds, no, thousands of years that make up the Age of Hala, so I really cannot afford to lose my way, can I?

I, an immortal, will be called to walk with mortal feet upon mortal soil as no immortal has ever walked before. I will be called to play our ancient and most sacred game of Akahna in a way that no immortal has ever done before.

Am I willing to do all of this and to sacrifice my own eternal life if I fail?

As I look at myself in the water, I know that I, Iuzio, really have no choice. I know that I can do nothing other than work to regain what we once had and to take us out of this Great Age of Hala. For I know that I am the only immortal who has the whole story clearly defined, from its perilous beginning to its mysterious end.

Oh, it is so quiet here now, Chi, just as it always is. As the dying sun cuts sharply across the red landscape in front of me, all is still and all seems so right with the world.

And I would give anything for this peace to go on.

3

But there is a part of the sky that is still darkening on the far horizon. I can see it from the corner of my eye. And I know that the battles of the human spirit will not be swift, but long, arduous, merciless and purposeless.

So I am looking across a landscape that will one day become unrecognisable. And it is a great sadness to me that all of this is destined to change. I see great empires and colossal dwellings rising up out of nowhere, cracking the earth as they soar up into the sky. I hear noise and chaos and loud monsters groaning where no monsters existed before. And I see sacred brooks and springs vanishing without trace, and a forgotten people buried beneath the rubble of countless civilisations. I squat here now where this rubble will one day be, knowing that there is already a way of life dying, daily, under my feet.

And I hear myself saying, 'Where has all that is good and true gone to?'

I speak these words to the water and I know that she hears me, as a fish leaps and creates a small wave.

Remember, Chi, that life will turn everything upside down, inside out and on its head. So, you see, we must always look at things as though they were face about. For that is the way the whole of nature understands them. We are then calling upon the good and the true that lie within them, and within ourselves.

Shadows will masquerade as you, Chi. But I will find you. I am determined to find you.

As I look at my reflection once again and see my face floating up from the depths, I bend to drink, cupping my hand in the water, as I always do at this hour of the day.

But my image disturbs me in a way it has never done before. I am shocked by what I see, because I not only see my troubled face, but a swirling dark cloud gathering behind me where no cloud should be. And I need to dip my hand into the water again to make ripples so that it fades.

And then I hear a chant upon the wind, coming from the place of the dark horizon, filling my ears with its dreadful monotonous moan. I hear something that people think is worthy, but which in reality is bringing on the most harmful curse the world has ever seen.

I shut my ears. I close my eyes.

I know what I have to do now.

And when I finally taste the water, it is sweet and pure, because I use my hand. But I would only need to look into a beaker, were I using one, to see the swirling dark cloud again, and if I were to drink it in, then I would be guaranteed an easier life in the future.

An easier life? Can there be an easier life?

This will certainly not be an easy fight, Chi.

I told you I have come here on so many occasions to listen to the stillness of the evening and to the song of the birds and to the trickling of the water, a sound that is like the tinkling of a hundred small bells in the wind and that I have loved for so long.

And suddenly I am crying for this. I am crying long, hard and loud. And my sobs are echoing about the beautiful wide landscape.

And as I catch a glimpse of my tear-stained face in the water, I also catch a glimpse of the One who is causing all of this to happen.

Why? I cry loudly. Why, my brother, did you need to do this?

* * * * *

The River of Life is long. It has no beginning and no end. Its currents will take us to places not of our choosing. Its hidden vortexes will carry us where we imagine we will never go.

When you meet this river you will be tempted to gaze upon your reflection. You will be lured to believe what you see.

So, will you look? Will you be pulled where you have vowed never to go? Beware as you stare into the liquid mirror, for the water is a clever mistress and her deception runs deep. And remember that we are each like a river that is searching for the sea, ever yearning for that something that is always somewhere just beyond us. For do not mortals long for a promise of eternity?

Yes. The mortal's thirst for power is strong and such an illusion will overshadow each and every soul if the flames of desire, envy and greed are fanned too well. So do not be tempted to gaze upon your reflection unless you mean to know who you really are.

I speak my words into many rivers, into many streams. And the words have already begun travelling along the currents, spinning within the eddies, flying up within the great waves, drying in the small droplets that lie in the sun.

Yes, this journey has already begun.

And my hope is that these words will be heard now, far and wide, across time and space, so that if you put your ear to the water you might hear my voice whispering where you expected to hear nothing at all. And I hope that this will dispel your pain, soothe your fear and cure your blindness. For, like a great blanket, the curse is destined to cover the whole earth and wipe our ancient memory away, and we must rediscover what is beneath and beyond.

So never allow the River of Life to lure you with its wondrous images. For should you become tempted by the dark illusory world you find in the water, you may just find yourself where the present chases the future and where the future can only ever chase the past. And you will become lost in shadow forever, like so many I have known and loved.

Journey with my hand in your hand. Know that I am by your side every minute of every day. For as I look at my own reflection beside this river in this dark hour, I, Iuzio the Immortal, pledge my soul to you, just as the stars pledge their souls to the night and the sun pledges his soul to the day. As our people are called to wander the earth to preserve our line and to find our true home in the west, I cast my own reflection far into the future, knowing that wherever you walk my footsteps will be in rhythm with yours and my heartbeat will be in harmony with yours.

Remember this. Remember me.
I, Iuzio, will be with you until our task is done.

The Eleventh Hala: The Near East

Horki's Tale

'When is gold not really gold?'

I give this riddle to my audience, some seated on the ground, some standing at the back. Around forty faces ponder the question.

I hold out a cupped hand. They crane their necks to look at the nugget of gold that is in my palm.

'Can't you see it?' I say.

Some pull at my fingers; they twist and turn my hand.

'Where is it?' they ask. 'Where is it?'

'I saw it,' one man yells loudly from the back of the crowd. 'I swear that I saw it, just now, with my very own eyes.'

'She keeps hiding it, of course,' another voice protests, 'because she doesn't want us to see it.'

'*I saw* it,' the man at the back insists, 'and it was a most beautiful sight.'

'Why can some of us see it and others not?' someone else asks.

'It is a strange magic that this girl performs,' another answers.

'All you have to do is look,' I tell them all, waving my palm under their noses again.

Then a woman sitting at the front gasps: 'There it is! I can see it. It's there. Now! Look! Such a beautiful nugget of gold.'

The rest crane to look, but again see nothing in my palm. And they are now *all* beginning to wonder what strange magic I am performing.

I smile at them. I have my fist clenched tightly around the nugget so that now no one is able to see it at all.

'Gold is a temptress,' I say. 'Gold is the mistress of illusion. But if you can answer the riddle I have given you, you will not only know the roots of illusion, but you may also get to understand the roots of beauty, power and wealth, and you will be able to see the nugget in your own palm when no one else can, as this man here just did, as this woman here just did.'

Once again I shoot the riddle out at the audience: 'When is gold not really gold? When is gold not really gold? When is gold not really gold?'

I repeat it three times so that its strong magic will increase. And those listening will either learn the lessons gold is trying to bring to them or they will find themselves on a lost path. The choice will be theirs.

Many are now scratching their heads. Some are asking the man and woman who saw my nugget to divulge the answer to the riddle. But the two shake their heads, determined they are not going to tell.

The crowd loves riddles, but they love the answers to riddles even more, especially when a powerful nugget of gold is at stake. If they want more clues, I tell them, they will have to return to the market-place tomorrow and bring more coins with them. There are more nuggets just like this one waiting to be found.

'Where?' many of them ask urgently.

I turn my face towards the blue haze that covers the distant mountains. And the audience cranes its neck and shields its eyes in the heat of the midday sun as it also looks in that direction. I see them all in my mind's eye, running to the mountains in their hunger for gold. I see them knocking each other over, cutting each other down as they frantically dig their fingers into the soil in their hunger for this precious metal.

At the beginning I told them that the nugget of gold made me a rich young woman in a very short time. I told them that the nugget had great magical power and gave me everything I ever desired: health, position, a handsome husband. But I also assured them that the answer to the riddle was the only key to finding these things.

'Do you really have this remarkable nugget? Or are you determined to perform some dark kind of magic on us?' one sensible man asks.

It is time for me to go, I think, because I have given them enough for today. It is also my way of ignoring the man's question.

I lift my hand and blow into my clenched fist, whispering some magical words, which a few in the crowd gasp at. I then throw my hand up in the air, as if releasing a bird. And I reveal that now there is nothing in my palm at all, and more people gasp as I turn to look again, wistfully, at the distant mountains. I tell them I have just sent my nugget skimming back across the land to that magnificent range where it belongs. There are whole families of nuggets in those mountains, I tell them, just waiting to hear the answer to the riddle.

Now there are a few sighs, a few boos, a few people saying, 'I told you all along that this was a trick.' But most are impressed. And really the little gold droplet is still in my hand. It's just that none of them are able to see it.

'Yes, it is gone now,' I tell them. 'It has become a part of those beautiful mountains again. And because I answered the riddle I can call this precious piece of gold to my side whenever I need it. I do not need to carry it in my purse. But know that it will be easier to throw yourself under the feet of wild horses, more desirable to hurl yourself into the flames of a fire than summon one of these nuggets to your side through the power of this ancient riddle.'

'Lies! Fairytales!' a heavily bearded man cries from the back of the crowd. He stands up and walks quickly away, his robe billowing behind him. But I know from his strong reaction that he believes every word I have just spoken. I also know that he wants to hear that it has been an easy task to acquire gold. He will be a man of one of these new religions that resist the laws of the Old Land.

Another man, old and ugly, is also distracting me. He is looking up at me with a glint in his eye and dribble on his chin. The carnal delights that gold can buy are luring him. I know that his soul is already lost. I know that if he were to look at his reflection in the polished surface of my nugget of gold, nothing but a squirming worm would be looking back at him.

'The reflection is a clever mistress and her deception runs deep,' I say, turning in his direction and repeating the words of a wise man. But I know he will not be able to hear me because he is enchanted by illusion and will be destined to serve his shadows forever. As he runs his eyes from my neck to my knees, Ag, the oldest of my seven brothers, is observing him closely from the back of the crowd.

My brother's arms are folded and he is leaning against a wall, chewing on a feathery strand of caraway, a herb that protects us from the bad magic we know is present within the crowd. We can smell the badness in the air. It gives us headaches. It gives us strange bouts of sickness. But Ag stays cool, calm. He knows the answer to the riddle. He knows what he is doing, just like my other brothers, who are also within the crowd.

I throw my blue veil across my shoulder in a dramatic gesture of confidence. Even though there is a disturbance among the people, I am self-assured, as all good storytellers must be. I am dressed in my best clothes, the brightest blue veil, bodice and leggings, so that I fit the part of a beautiful young woman who has known the splendours of gold and its powerful magic.

Many eyes hunger for this precious metal as they look at me: dark eyes, pale eyes, slant eyes, and one man with just one eye. But then I feel something touching my ankle. The old man's hand is caressing it. I pull my foot away, swiftly kicking him in the jaw at the same time, which makes another woman giggle.

'Cross my palm, sir, lady. Make yourself lucky!' I hear one of my sisters crying urgently.

She passes into the crowd, attempting to distract everyone from the blow I have just delivered. Her palm is under their noses. And my second sister joins her. Our hands are always under people's noses. People know that to place silver in the palm of an Egyptian is to invite the greatest luck. And everyone is desperate for luck.

After paying us handsomely, everyone trickles away, some saying the riddle to themselves, all desperate to know the answer. But the old man lingers, leering up at me. Life's riddles do not interest him. I might have kicked him from one end of the market-place to the other and still he would be leering. I don't know where he comes from, as such a variety of people congregate here in this town. He has tanned skin, a plain turban and plain white robe, but so does everyone else. I imagine he is from the south. We never trust anyone from the south. They are wealthy, loud, forceful people. They have many bad spirits living within them. They will cut you down as soon as look at you.

We are counting out our money. We have made a lot today. And Ag is moving forward and soon squatting down beside the old man. Our other brothers linger protectively, spreading out, staying alert.

Ag is twelve years my senior. At thirty-two he is a striking sight to the women, with his black curly hair, his dark beard, his yellow shirt open at the chest and his baggy white leggings. I notice some of the women ogling him, imagining him lying on top of them.

Ag wears protective colourful beads, gold at his throat and red wool around his wrists and ankles, as we all do. He wears kohl around his eyes and henna on his palms and on the soles of his feet, as we all do. We protect ourselves by adorning ourselves with anything that will bring us luck. We carry herbs and spices. We smell very sweet and beautiful. We know how important it is to have luck on our side in these towns where anything can happen and everything can go wrong.

Ag is still chewing on the sprig of caraway as he is talking to the old man. I will always love and admire my eldest brother.

'You are keen on my sister then?' he says.

The old man sees that my brother is serious and expresses his excitement. He laughs. It is a disgusting laugh, which only those from the south can make, and to my horror my brother is actually egging him on and they are ogling me together. It is no longer a joke. It is suddenly going too far.

'How much would you give me for this girl then?' my brother asks in his quiet confident manner, fingering his beard.

The old man is thinking about this and I am horrified as I watch him dipping into his purse. Beads of perspiration are forming on his brow at the thought of getting his hands on me. And my brother is eager to start the bargaining.

In anger I push Ag away, cuffing his ears and shouting obscenities at him in our native tongue. But he is strong and holds my arms down, reprimanding me with his eyes.

The contents of the old man's purse are emptied into my brother's palms and I am unable to believe what I am seeing. I have always trusted Ag so much.

Ag is putting a little of the money into his own purse and tying it at his waist. He has very delicate fingers, which I used to admire. He has a charming way, which I used to admire. I admire nothing about him any more.

He is talking to the old man all the while, his eyebrows going up and down, a grin on his face as he tells him how good I am in bed, and how I will dance for him

13

whenever music is played, and how he will be able to show me off to all his friends.

'This girl is well worth the money,' he assures him.

My other brothers are soon closing in, helping their brother to seal the deal. I am thinking that now they are *all* going to turn against me.

Ag spreads the remainder of the money between them, as if paying them for their services. And the old man rubs his hands together in delight, salivating as he looks me over.

I am betrayed. I cannot believe that this has happened.

But then my brother draws a great breath, holding it for a while, with all of us watching him.

And soon he cries: 'Akahna!'

And suddenly we all take off together, scattering in many directions, my brother pulling me along by the hand, my sister galloping in front of us, leaping high with excitement. She loves this game because she is never the one who is sold. My other sister and brothers have all run in different directions so that no one will ever know who has most of the money.

We run through the narrow streets, knocking into stalls and barrows, knocking into asses who bray in disgust. People shout curses upon us and wave their fists as we fly past them. Our shadows race beside us in the strong sunlight. We know that the ancient game of Akahna is a dangerous game, but my brother has been schooled by his elders and plays it with the greatest of skill. Even though men with sticks may chase us, even though we may be stoned from a village or town, we would trust no one more than Ag to help us flee from a dangerous situation.

We reach the brow of the hill at the edge of the town and move off the wide dry dusty road, all of us catching our breath, all of us clutching our sides with laughter. We call out names, we make rude signs, we mimic the old man. We know he will not have given chase. He hasn't the energy to walk, let alone run.

14

And we also mimic the audience who could not see my nugget of gold. Very few people can see my nugget of gold. My brothers and sisters, when merged with an audience, will swear that they can see it, at my prompting. But do they see it really?

I know you will be asking now: 'Do you really see this nugget of gold yourself, Horki? Is it real?'

That will be for you to decide, Chi, once I have given you the whole story. For it is then that I will invite you to look into my palm. And who knows what you will see?

I have soon kissed Ag on the cheek for playing such a wonderful game of Akahna. We Egyptian women are proud of our men when they play the game well. Ag is a clever man. In a crowd he knows who is likeable and who isn't, who has a soul and who doesn't. If there is an unpopular, wealthy, soulless halfwit whose pocket could be picked several times over, Ag will know that he can safely sell his sister to that man for a generous sum.

And we have all learned that we must believe in what we are doing if we are to have success with any of our games. All will go smoothly if I believe that Ag is going to sell me, as it will if Sonna, my eldest sister, believes that she is going to lose me – she is good at dropping to her knees and pulling on Ag's shirt. And all will go smoothly if Rupe, my second eldest sister, believes that all hope is lost – she is good at bursting into floods of tears.

My brothers always close in on us, showing that they are on Ag's side, protecting the deal, silently letting the buyer know that he can trust them and that they are not going to let me escape. And by this time most of the audience will have gone. I will have played my part in bringing them together, which will have enabled Ag to single someone out.

We have to work together. If we do not act our parts well we will not only subject ourselves to danger but we will not be playing the game of Akahna in its most ancient and sacred form.

Yes, this game is ancient and sacred and has been played by all our ancestors. When Ag gives the signal to run, we offer up prayers to our ancestors for delivering us into this blessed position and for teaching us this precious game.

Each time Ag cries, 'Akahna!' we are filled with ecstasy, and our souls and our legs are suddenly flying.

Akahna is mostly a boy's game and takes many forms. A boy who reaches puberty will need to take something, usually gold, silver or a valuable stone, from a halfwit, or gaujo, in order to become initiated as a man. All seven of my brothers have done this. The gaujos are those religious people who have fallen under a bad spell and become greedy. They have no wisdom within them. They are blinded by their passions and illusions, fooled by the reflections they see whenever they look at themselves, fooled by the magic of gold. They cannot be trusted, because their deception runs deep. And our elders, especially our women, say that those who will go searching for the smallest nugget of gold in a vast range of mountains, those who will buy a girl in a market-place without conscience, deserve to have the game of Akahna played upon them over and over again, until their souls hurt.

Gaujos will rob gold from the earth and give it to people. We will rob gold from people and give it back to the earth. We keep a little gold for good luck and a little for trading. But it doesn't follow that the more gold you have, the more good luck you have.

Ag would never sell me. He would lay down his life before he would exchange me for gold. He knows that if ever he plays the game badly he will have my father to answer to. I have sometimes wished I were a boy so that I could play Akahna as well as our menfolk do.

My father has said that our sacred game will serve these halfwits well if they will only learn that taking from the earth for one's own ends is the same as robbing one's own grandmother. You will earn trouble, not luck, if you rob your own grandmother. He says that they will call our

16

people thieves and rogues, but who is doing the stealing?

If we use gold wisely, as our ancestors did, we know that we will never become cursed by it. An ancestor told us that those who are bewitched by gold are destined to lose their souls forever.

You will be wondering how it is we know these things.

Well, we know these things because we are the cleverest actors, the most creative storytellers, the most cunning tricksters, the most skilled liars. We are proud of being Egyptians – even though we are not Egyptians. Some people call us Gypsies. And we will be Egyptians, or Gypsies, for as long as anyone wants us to be.

It is strange that if people do not know where you come from they will decide for themselves where that place is.

When I look out of my tent to the great mountains I am glad that I still remember where the Old Land really is. It is within the blue veil of mist upon the mountains in the west; it is concealed in those places where the bird soars and where heat hazes shimmer; it is beyond every ocean, behind the sky and beyond all those places we can never quite see. And that is why I send my gold nugget back to the mountains in the west every evening, with a prayer. For there is nowhere better for my nugget to be. The misty veils will guard and protect it, just as the blue misty veil I wear guards and protects me.

Yes, we are a mystery to people, because we are beings who understand the language of gold, the language of the Otherworld and woodland spirits and little people and dragons and the wisest of men. It has even been suggested that some of us are nature spirits in disguise. It has also been suggested that we journey west to make it look as though we originated from this physical world after all, because everyone is compelled to move west or east along the main routes connecting these two important directions.

And we tell everyone – really because they keep telling us – that we are wanderers from the land of Egypt, because Egypt seems to be the most otherworldly and mystical place that anyone has ever heard of. And we tell them we are journeying back to that place as we move west.

My father, who is a holy man and who knows many things and who has long had visions about the past and the future, used to say to me: 'Our homeland is beyond a great water. Our homeland will be found where we are able to fall off the edge of the land in the place where the sun sits down in the west.'

And so we long for this great water to draw near, as that is bound to take us closer to the Old Land.

And it has been said many times that we Egyptians can enter the Otherworld by falling off the edge of the horizon, because the sun falls into the Otherworld in the same way every night. And our people consider it sensible to follow the path of the sun. The sun is a lover of the moon. And my father says that by the time we find the water and step across it we will have become so like the sun that the moon will part the waves of her waters and will be begging us to move within her so that we can cross to the other side.

Remember that to fall off the edge of the land purposefully is to enter the Otherworld skilfully, with your soul intact, as the sun does. This is what our wisest elders say. They also say that to fall by accident, stumbling on a rock on the road or simply tripping over something, means you could risk falling by someone else's hand. So if we do not take care, we could enter the Otherworld under some kind of enchantment and risk losing our souls forever.

And what would we do then?

So I do not want to trip up on the road. I have no desire to become enchanted. I would rather keep my soul. We have always taken every care to step along the road with our eyes open wide, because the road is long and it is all we have.

For a long time many of my people were unable to understand how we could all fall off the edge of the land into such a vast stretch of water all together at the same time, as my father had suggested. But my father explained that in his vision there was a sheet of pure blue silk and it was being stretched out across the earth by invisible spirit hands. Sometimes this sheet was smooth, other times silver coins were being tossed upon it like a great many dancing stars. He said that when it was being shaken by all those unseen hands, billowing and ballooning so beautifully, he couldn't take his eyes off it. He knew we would all somehow have to fall upon it together so that we could all fall off it together when we reached the other side. He didn't know at the time that he had seen an ocean. And nobody else knew he had seen an ocean, until one day an elder was recounting a story about the sea, and then everyone realised exactly what my father had seen.

But many of the old ones still prefer to believe that they will one day walk across a sheet of silk bearing dancing stars.

There are naturally a few in our tribe who question our passage west because it appears to take us no nearer to our destination. There was a time when we moved north, south and east as well. But most believe it is safest to keep to the sun's path now that the world is changing so rapidly and so many are losing their souls. It is also thought that with our horses, asses, carts and tents we are simply doing what we have been doing for thousands of years: trading as we move, entertaining as we move and fortune-telling as we move. So if we continue moving and doing all these things we will keep ourselves safe and all will be well.

But so many are now travelling along the main routes west and east that we think they too must be questioning their destination. We see merchants, traders of all kinds, bandits, beggars, holy men, masters with slaves, slaves without masters, people from the east with slant eyes, people from the west with hair as red and wild as fire, people with skin as black as the night, people with skin as white as sunlight upon white stone, mule trains and camel caravans and elephant processions, and all moving as if part of a great snake, weaving sometimes in one direction and sometimes in the other.

And the very worst travellers of all are those from the south with teeth. Yes, those I have already spoken about, those who have many shadows in their huge white teeth and who will show you their teeth purposefully to try to bewitch you. They will terrorise, rob or kill you if they can. And they will do it all with their teeth.

But do any of these travellers within the snake really know where they are going? So many of them are moving in their sleep, we are not sure. Much of the time this human snake is not really moving at all, because none of the people who are part of it are awake. And so they are not moving in their souls. They want to become rich. They would rather travel to find a small nugget of gold somewhere in a vast range of mountains than travel to find their destiny. That is the way the world has become. That is the spell that gold casts if we succumb to the spirit of greed.

I hope it is better in the future.

Sometimes we grow weary because we are always travelling, travelling, travelling. Sometimes we think we are no better than the next person who is just ahead in the giant snake or just behind, and we wonder if we will ever meet the edge of the land.

My father has fallen off the edge of the land many times in his dreams and he has left his body sitting under the stars, so that it is still sitting there in the same position in the morning. And when he returns to speak to us, his voice has become full of stardust. And so we learn how stars talk to each other. The stars are our ancestors who have risen up to the heavens after death, having earned themselves an honoured place in the sky. So to hear them speaking is a wonderful thing.

But gaujos do not understand this and in these dangerous times we overhear them, from the smallest market-place to the greatest stretch of desert, saying, 'Never trust an Egyptian, no matter what he tells you. Egyptians tell lies and fairytales and live in fantasy.'

And gaujos will also say: 'How does one Egyptian

ever manage to live with another?'

They do not understand us. They do not believe that people who live in fantasy and who tell lies might also live in harmony. They do not understand us because we see truth in what they think of as untruth and untruth in what they think of as truth.

So now I have told you all of this, now that we have come this far, I will sometimes question you to ensure that you are worthy of this knowledge. It isn't easy to think the way we Egyptians do. We make it hard. Remember that I too have been questioned many times, by my elders, by my ancestors, to ensure that I carry my knowledge in the wisest way.

So ask yourself this now: Do you believe that the blind man is blind? Do you believe that the cripple is lame? Or do you believe that the man who sees could be blind and that those who have legs could be lame?

Think about this.

And can you understand the following riddle: What needs to be beloved and true and hateful and venomous all at the same time? (You will need to remember and think about this.)

And yes: When is gold not really gold?

We Egyptians like our riddles, because we believe that nothing is ever as it seems. Most gaujos fear our riddles. And most halfwits will never believe that the answer to this riddle is a riddle in itself: *Gold is not gold when it is also copper.*

If you cannot tell the difference between copper and gold and silver and gold and silver and copper, how will you know a substitute when you see one? Because the sacred metals will all have merged into one. And you will be left with nothing but fool's gold.

So we could also say that gold is not gold when it is also silver. And silver is not silver when it is also gold. And your head might just be your feet.

Am I getting through to you, Chi? Are you hearing what I am saying?

21

You see, the world has lost its magical understanding and its links with the spirits of sacred metals; it has lost the Otherworld. But you'll discover the wisdom behind these words, I hope, as you remember. Yes, you must at all times allow your soul to *remember*.

I want to tell you now that if you ever lose your links with your true place of birth, the Otherworld, and all that is associated with the Otherworld, you will lose your life. Remember this, because it is important. Each and every one of us is looking for our true homeland. Each and every one of us is running across the land, desperate to reunite with our soul, running and running. And we don't realise when we are doing so much running that we are leaving our souls far behind us. We risk falling off the edge of the land by accident. We risk never coming back. So never run that hard, Chi, because I have heard that the great chasms of the Lowerworld are packed with fallen people.

There is a lot for you to learn. And you will hear me telling you over and over again that deception runs deep. You will grow tired of hearing me say this. But it needs to be said. And when I say it I will be speaking the words as I heard them spoken by the wise man, the ancestor I need to tell you about, because he is the one who taught me to remember.

* * * * *

The wise man's name is Iuzio. And he is the one who gave me the gold nugget. But I cannot tell you about him without first telling you about the nugget and about the art of reflection.

The nugget is wonderful to touch. It is so smooth you could be touching silk or air. It has the power to transport you to places you never dreamed you would go. You can hold the nugget to your face and it will caress you. You can rub it on your skin and it will heal you. Sung to under the full moon, it will bring you a husband or wife. I like to smell the nugget, taste the nugget, because I am so passionate about it. And there was a time when I would gladly have eaten it, had it been edible.

Yes, gold is that delicious.

And most of us can feel this way, Chi, because we have desired gold since earth and sky were young and we first learned to walk between them. It is easy to become tempted and you must keep your wits about you, because the spirit of gold knows a halfwit when she sees one. And if you begin to feel the saliva gathering in your mouth and your tongue moving over your lips, beware.

You see, we always want to gobble up those things we fall in love with, and too many of us fall head over heels with the spirit of gold. So, if we feel that yearning inside us, that hungering, we must listen to our spirits and understand what is happening to us.

Iuzio taught me the art of being carried away by gold, and by all that shines, a long time ago. He encouraged me to polish the nugget so that I could see my reflection in its surface. And as long as I saw myself as I was, I would never fall prey to gold's darker side.

So I hope I can teach you this now too, Chi: how to polish your reflection, how to respect gold, how not to gobble up the things you fall in love with. I want to teach you all these important things.

But first, you should know that the art of polishing is an ancient art and that people learned to polish their reflections a long time ago. In the days when the earth was new they polished, and in the days when there were no towns or great cities they polished; they polished in the deserts and in the hills and along the trade routes.

Everyone polished.

And to understand what the word 'reflection' means you will need to go back to those early times and to realise that no one was looking for a face in the water back then, but for what was beyond a face.

We Egyptians still practise this ancient art today; we are still looking for the memories of our people which are contained within the great River of Life, which we call the Boro Dikimangro. And these two words mean 'Long Reflection', Chi, and these will probably be the most important two words you will ever learn.

You see, all that is shiny, all that can dazzle us, remembers. And water remembers best. And so you must take care when you are in the presence of water. You must treat the spirit of water with the greatest respect. Egyptians understand that if they entrust their most treasured personal memories to the greater memory that is within water, and treat water with respect at the same time, they will always be protected.

Yes, our people leave their reflections in the river as you might leave your mark upon the bark of a tree or upon stone; we are saying: 'I was here.' And all these reflections can be found at any time in any river if we know where to look for them and how to pluck them out of the water.

Yes, Chi, anyone who has ever looked into a river has their reflection contained there.

That is something that is hard to believe, isn't it?

Our reflections will be left floating in the rivers as long as there is water flowing on the earth. And as the rivers swell and they all run into each other all across the world, so the reflections move and travel, sometimes together, sometimes apart.

Look, when you are sitting beside a river, Chi, and you may see reflections passing by, some that were cast into the rivers a long time ago, perhaps thousands of years ago, along with those that were cast just yesterday. You may not be able to tell where or when they were cast. But when you learn how to *look*, you will know them.

And should you allow yourself to become that little bit greedy, like the slobbering old man in the market-place, you may just end up plucking his reflection out of the water when you meant to pluck out something nice. Because greed attracts more greed. And those greedy reflections are sweeping along with the more genuine ones. And we always pluck out those reflections that are

24

identical to our own. Don't we?

So, do not become greedy, Chi. It is not worth becoming greedy only to find yourself wearing the grimace of a slobbering old man.

Polish your reflection hard whenever you look at yourself, until it is clear and true. Never give up refining who you are. If you do not have a nugget of gold, you will need to use a looking-glass.

By the time I was old enough to start looking into water properly, I was beginning to know what I was all about. I was looking into many shiny surfaces – into silver, into copper, into mirrors – understanding that the more clearly I could see myself, the more inner wealth I was destined to find.

So, consider these questions now also, Chi: Who can separate out all the raindrops in the ocean once they have fallen into it? Who can separate out all the reflections in a river?

This makes you think, Chi, doesn't it?

The wise man I spoke of told me all about this.

You see, your face will be reflected in the river, as will a tree and the sky and a bird and the sunlight and all that is around you. And just as we cannot separate out all the raindrops, so we will not be able to separate out all the reflections. You will begin to realise that there is absolutely nowhere along the river that does not contain a reflection.

And there isn't, is there?

Where would we be if every river contained just one raindrop? Where would we be if every river contained just one reflection?

Think about this as well. You see, whether we are talking about raindrops or reflections, they all get to travel across the world, in their many thousands.

So, ask yourself this now, also: Where do the raindrops go after they have dropped into the water? Are they all collected on the surface? Or do they all sink down into the depths?

A younger cousin of mine once said to me: 'Why do

you keep talking of raindrops, Horki? Why don't you talk about the more important things in life?'

And I told her that raindrops *are* the important things in life when they are giving us clues about our ancient River of Life, our identity and our ancient heritage. They are important if they are helping us to learn where our spirits have travelled from and where they are travelling to.

So, just as you, and my cousin, may not know where a raindrop goes, and may not even care where a raindrop goes, neither will you know where your reflection goes after you have looked in the water.

You probably never even thought of that before, did you?

Remember that one reflection, like one raindrop, merges into many. They all come together, performing their own dances and singing their own songs, and then they live in a world of their own, just as we do when we get close to each other and love each other and merge together.

And if you don't believe me, go to the nearest river and you will see for yourself how raindrops do this when they fall. Follow a raindrop down from the sky. Don't lose sight of it. And then see if you can spot where it has landed after it has fallen into the water.

It will be hard to focus on that one raindrop alone. You will find that you can only imagine where it might have gone. And before you know it, it will have taken on a life of its own, dancing in the waves and currents, singing in the foam.

You will need to remember that raindrops, once cast into a river, will reunite with each other and with their own ancient memories. And when you cast your reflection into the river, the same thing will occur. So when you look beyond your face in the river, you will be likely to see the faces of all your people stretching from beginning to end: the whole of your ancestral line.

That's something even more interesting to think about, isn't it, Chi?

And, Chi, know that I have sometimes been able to

see your reflection looking back at me from the river, even though you are not yet born.

You have been there in the future because your reflection has been cast by your greater soul: the soul of our ancestral line. And you wear an expression of bewilderment, like so many in the future. You have a fear of things that belong to the inner world. And if I am truthful, I am afraid that you may just fall down into the chasm of the Lowerworld if you do not take the time to understand your inner world.

Yes, my biggest fear, Chi, is that no one will follow you in our line and that you may just end up being the last of us.

I sometimes don't know what to do about this fear.

I hope I am going to be wrong.

So, I say now, as I say my own name loudly, firmly, and as I see myself in my own reflection: 'Horki, have courage and stay strong. You must have hope for the future, for Chi's future. And you must remember the valuable lessons you have learned about beauty, wealth and power. Because you can pass this knowledge on to Chi and that will ultimately help the ancestral line to continue to flow within the River of Life. And perhaps there will not be an end after all.'

Yes, it is sometimes a dark future that I see. But I do not want to pass these fears on to the face that I see, even though this face is often barely an outline. I cannot even tell if you are a boy or a girl, Chi, when I am talking to you. All I know is that I love you very much and that in your soul you must be beautiful.

They told me I was beautiful a long time ago. When old women looked at me they mourned their youth and when young women looked at me they were filled with envy, because I was destined to radiate beauty wherever I went. And that is why beauty came to teach me a great lesson.

I think of that beauty now as I look over the water and see a blur that quickly becomes my face. I see my thick gold nose-ring, worn to protect me, ballooning out from my nostril. I see the silver coins glistening in my dark hair, like bright stars peppering the edge of a thick black cloud.

So I need to tell you now about beauty, power and wealth, Chi, because I need to help you learn about gold's darker side. For when we look into the Boro Dikimangro it is easy to become dazzled by all that shines.

You need to know too that Iuzio was very handsome, so handsome that whenever he looked into the water, Pahni, the spirit of water, was herself dazzled by his beauty, especially by his eyes, which were bluer than the bluest of her waters and deeper than the deepest of her oceans. And she is never lured easily by any mortal or immortal.

And all the reflections in the river saw this and those that were as bad as the slobbering old man gathered together and tried to take Iuzio's soul away, because they were so envious. Yes, they tried to carry his image away down the river so that they could be rid of it. But this caused them problems, because he was such a lucky and powerful being, as well as an immortal. He was, and still is, a very special spirit.

So he remained strong and because he respected Pahni she was inspired to help him with his task. And this great water spirit gave him a vision one day when he looked, a vision about our line ending and about the curse of mankind and the many things that I have been talking to you about. And this curse of mankind was also known as the Boro Hukni, or Great Lie or Great Trick. It is a spell of the very worst kind, Chi, a spell that was laid by a great and wicked sorcerer many thousands of years ago, a sorcerer who understood the nature of reflections and the nature of lies and tricks and beauty and wealth and power.

This sorcerer had a passion to change the world for good, Chi. In his spell he willed that people would forget who they were. They would lose their memories over thousands of years so that when they looked in the rivers they would no longer know what they were looking for.

And if this evil sorcerer could make us forget so much then he could replace ancient memory with strange dark memories which were not associated with our past at all, though we would believe that they were. And these false memories would give beauty, power and wealth very different meanings.

And his curse didn't take long to take effect, Chi, for as soon as it had been laid, people started looking at their reflections differently. And they started not to mind what they saw. And there was nothing anyone could do about that, because a strong part of the curse was to believe that the curse was broken when it wasn't. And you could hear this sorcerer laughing in the woodland, laughing in the wilderness, laughing in the dead of night, because to him it was all so funny.

And if you have ever tried to break a curse that is unbreakable you will know the kind of curse I am talking about, Chi. You will need to work very hard if you want to do anything about it, because for the rest of eternity you may just find yourself shrugging at everything and saying, 'Ah, never mind.'

But then this spell also decreed that people would end up forgetting their own voices, so that when they spoke, strange sounds would come out of their mouths, harsh and grating, shouting all across the world, making all the trees and animals and wise ones stop their ears. And they would no longer recognise their own faces, so that when they looked at themselves they would not know who they were any more.

This sorcerer could fix another face into their reflections so easily, you see. People would look into the water and would see whatever they desired to see – or whatever the sorcerer desired them to see.

And the sorcerer himself had cast nine images into the river for anyone to pluck out. Yes, nine, Chi. That is the worst kind of evil magic. For who would ever need to abuse the spirit of number nine in such a way?

And now everyone dances to those nine reflections

all across the world. Yes, they are dancing without knowing they are dancing, because they have all at some time plucked out one of these images and been affected by its bad magic.

Did you ever wonder why so many people's faces look the same, Chi?

Iuzio saw that these distorted reflections would eventually turn people to stone and dust and shadow, which was just what the evil sorcerer wanted so that he could fulfil his own dark destiny. So if you happened to become one of these dust-shadow people, Chi, you would never see yourself properly again and you would never properly live again. Nor would you die.

In fact, if this was your fate, you would remain cursed dust and shadow forever more, with people walking all over you and grinding you down, so much so that you would no longer know what was happening, nor how it was happening. And you wouldn't be able to tell the difference between substance and shadow, night and day, white and black, yes and no, and so on, in fact all that is positive and negative.

And still you would be saying, 'Ah, never mind.'

I hear so many in the future saying these three familiar words, Chi.

So Iuzio made a vow to help our people, because this almighty shadow was walking our way. And our beloved ancestor needed to make a sacrifice if he wanted to do something about it. And so he promised to devote himself to guiding our people back to their real home in the Otherworld by helping us all follow the safe path of the sun.

And he *will* help us, Chi. We have to believe that he will.

So you will find that while it is common to have a guide in your life, helping you to reunite with your destiny, it is not so common to be working against such a great and terrible curse as the one that has been thrown over the world. We must stick together now, more than ever, because times are going to be difficult over the many hundreds of years that lie ahead.

And just as you learn the name of Iuzio, so you must also learn the name of Beng now, Chi. For this is the name of the wicked sorcerer I speak of. And you should not use his name lightly, for it is not the sort of thing one does. You will hear your ancient grandmother pouring curses upon this name over and over again, and spitting three times, and sometimes even nine times, every time she hears his name mentioned.

And, Chi, if there is damage in your world in your time, you will know who to blame. If bad luck enters your life in your time you will know who to blame.

Remember also, Chi, that Beng has mastered the art of turning himself into anything he wants to. And he is known as the Boro Mulo, the Great Vampire, to all our people. And should you ever fall under his masterful spell, you may not see how fond he is of eating things alive until it is too late. You will have such blind admiration for him that you will lose yourself to him completely.

And that is why Iuzio calls the gaujo world the Blind World, because people have so much dust in their eyes and ears that they do not see or hear what is happening to them. They have all lost their senses.

Stay away from too much dust, Chi. Stay away from too many shadows. Never walk out when the wind blows too hot or too strong. Never walk down the edge of a street, but down its centre.

And Beng uses his children to get to you. Your ancient grandmother very nearly walked into Beng through one of his children, in and out, like the sun disappearing and reappearing from behind a dark cloud. I was regurgitated by this great monster because he couldn't stomach me – which was a good thing, because once Beng has eaten you, it is usually the end of you. So trust that your ancient grandmother knows what Beng is all about.

And still I have bad dreams about the time good and bad fought out their terrible battle within me, when I very nearly turned to dust and shadow overnight. Without Iuzio's help, I would have changed into the harshest piece of stone, the grittiest grain of dust.

So it is time now to tell you about this, and I must tell you how I met Iuzio and how I found the golden nugget.

* * * * *

I was around six years old and playing in the sun beside some rocks when I first met our beloved ancestor. One of the rocks was extremely warm to touch. And I was patting it with the flat of my hand when I heard it say, 'Ouch!'

I looked up and saw a man sitting beside a fire, a man with hair that was red like fire and eyes that were blue like the sky, those deep blue eyes I have already told you about. They were big, like two blue pools stretching away from me towards a place I didn't know but thought I could touch if I stretched my hand out far enough. And he had the most alluring smile. He was wearing a rusty hooded robe and creamy-coloured leggings and sandals, and had a brown shawl thrown carelessly around his shoulders. And he was sitting cross-legged, idly poking his fire with a stick.

'Did I hurt the rock?' I wanted to know, worried that this man might reprimand me.

'No, Horki,' he said, with amusement in his voice.

He knew my name. But I didn't know how, because I didn't know him.

'The rock talked,' I told him eagerly.

'Yes, Horki,' he answered. 'All rocks talk. You'll be able to hear them talk if you listen to them hard enough.'

'Chakani talks,' I giggled, carrying this a little further, mostly out of embarrassment, as I held my dolly up to his ear. She was made out of bits of bright material sewn together by my mother and aunt. She was my special sister, adviser and friend. Chakani means 'star' and she was named after the brightest star in the sky, which sometimes directed our path. She had plenty of kohl around her eyes to protect her, her hair was lucky because it was taken from our horses' tails, she had red wool wound around her small

32

wrists, neck and feet, which gave her even more luck and helped to keep her alive, and she had a bright pink veil flowing out from her head, so she was a grown-up woman as well as a star from the sky.

'Chakani tells me many secrets,' I told the man.

'Chakani tells me she enjoys being with you,' he said, listening to her speaking in his ear. 'She says you count the stars together at night.'

I nodded, because this was true, and it proved to me that Chakani was really talking to him, because he couldn't possibly have known this on his own. Chakani and I counted the stars every night because the stars were our human ancestors and I wanted to know how many ancestors I had.

So I asked the man, 'How many stars are there in the sky?'

'As many as there are raindrops,' he said.

'And how many raindrops are there?'

'As many as there are stars in the sky.'

I thought this made sense.

'How do you know my name?'

He smiled at me, seeming to be amused.

'Because I too am a star,' he said. 'And stars know things that humans don't.'

I gasped. 'Are you really a star from up in the sky?' I asked, widening my eyes.

He nodded, still looking into his fire.

I moved closer to him and looked into the fire to see what he might be looking at in the flames. He seemed very big and his fiery red hair seemed to be made out of the flames themselves, while his deep blue eyes seemed to be made out of the sky, for you could look into them and fly somewhere far away. I looked upon him as being part fire, part sky. And this made me laugh because it seemed funny. I had never seen a man with red hair before and I had never seen a man with blue eyes before. Chakani had never seen these things either. But we agreed that this man seemed like one of our own people, because his skin was tanned like ours, and because of the way he was. We thought it exciting that we were sharing a campfire with a real star.

'What's your name?' I asked him. 'Do stars have names?'

'Some do and some don't,' he answered. 'Usually, if we are boy stars we are given our names by the sky and the sun, and if we are girl stars we are given our names by the earth and the moon. I was given the name Iuzio by the sky and the sun a very long time ago, and then when I came down to the earth to walk about on it just like you, I was given a different name, Perri. But when my grandfather the sky and my father the sun wanted me back again, they called me back to sit in the sky and then I became Iuzio again. And I've been living up in the sky for so long now that my eyes have turned blue like the sky and my hair has turned red like the sun. But I have now earned the honour of going back and forth from sky to earth whenever I please.'

I frowned.

'Does it hurt to come down from the sky?' I asked very seriously, remembering the times I had fallen over when I had jumped down from the rocks.

He smiled affectionately. 'No, Horki, it doesn't hurt.'

I knew he was amused with me again. So I hit him affectionately and Chakani hit him affectionately and I was going to ask him some more questions about the lives of stars when I saw something very shiny in his hand. And my eyes widened when I saw a beautiful nugget of gold, about the size of a small egg, in his flattened palm.

'This is for you, Horki,' he told me. 'You must guard this nugget well. You must polish it as you grow older and you must make sure you only ever polish it yourself. You must keep looking into the nugget until you see yourself as you really are, because a lesson is going to come to you about the temptations of gold and what is going to happen in the future, a lesson about wealth and beauty and power. So, when you look at yourself in the River of Life, you must remember that the water is a clever mistress and her deception runs deep.'

I was excited about this, although I didn't know what he was talking about. But I carried the nugget away with me, then ran back to him so that I could throw my arms around his neck for giving me such a wonderful present. I kissed his cheek and felt its smooth warmth, and Chakani kissed his cheek and felt the warmth too. And then we both ran back to the rock, scrambled half over it and turned to give our friend a final wave.

But the man with the red hair and blue eyes, the man who was a star, had vanished.

And to this day, Chi, I believe that he must have gone straight back up into the sky.

* * * * *

When I returned to my camp I was reprimanded by my elders. My mother shook me angrily, telling me that there were bandits everywhere and I could have been taken away or sold as a slave or even killed. I told them all I'd just been for a walk and didn't mention that I'd talked to an ancestor, a real star from up in the sky. I hid the nugget of gold and only took it out when no one was watching. And I could not return to the place where I had met Iuzio until many days later. My two elder sisters had orders to accompany me wherever I went.

When I went back there was no sign of Iuzio, not even a sign that a fire had been laid in that place. I had told my two sisters about Iuzio and they were sworn to secrecy, but I had mentioned nothing to them about the golden nugget. They explained to me that the man I had met must have been a spirit of the rocks who had come out to play with me through boredom. But I knew the truth.

Our tribe eventually moved away and I mourned Iuzio, and developed a fascination for rocks. As I grew into puberty I was allowed to wander on my own, so that one day when I found some rocks forming a small cave, I was

35

naturally tempted to explore them.

But on closer examination I realised I was looking into a wide mouth set in a grin. A tangle of bushes surrounded it, looking like hair standing on end with a heavy beard and moustache beneath. I laughed and was filled with dread at the same time, wondering if I was peering into the mouth of a man from the south whose teeth were the rocks themselves.

The desire to see Iuzio again was strong, though, so I was driven to fight my way through the thorny overgrowth, catching myself on prickles and releasing myself from many clinging vines.

Here was a great test for me, Chi. Here was pure desire running wild, which up until this time I'd had no consciousness of. And the closer I got to the cave, the more I was beginning to hear the warning my little nugget was giving me.

'Step no further, Horki, step no further,' she kept telling me.

'The darkness conceals the light,' I could also hear my father saying as I went on blindly.

'But does the light conceal the darkness?' I had asked him one day in return. He had given me an answer to that question and it had been very wise, but as I entered the cave, I was unable to recall exactly what he had said. Perhaps he knew I would one day have to find the answer for myself by fighting my way into a dark cave.

Understand that I didn't know a great deal about the subject of darkness at this time, Chi, and I knew even less about light. I was just thirteen, and darkness and light were merely part of the elders' campfire stories that I had caught through the mists of dreams as I was falling asleep.

Now as I entered the cave I was intent on seeing Iuzio there. I was expecting to see Iuzio there.

'Do you still have the nugget, Horki?' I heard a voice say.

I turned in the direction of the voice, but I could see no one. Darkness surrounded me. But there was the voice, loud in the air, and my excitement grew.

'Of course I have the nugget,' I said, taking it out of its purse, which I kept tied at my hips. 'I polish it daily, just as you said I should. And I am beginning to look at myself, just as you said I should.'

'Take care, Horki, take care,' my little nugget was saying.

Then I realised that the owner of the voice had started walking up and down. I could hear his feet going past. I could see his shadow moving across the cave wall. It was large, as if cast by the flames of a well-fuelled fire, yet the only light was the faint light of the moon outside.

I noticed that the man seemed to be thinking as he walked. His arms were folded; his shoulders were hunched. His shadow looked like the kind of shadow Iuzio's body would cast. And the lilt in his voice was Iuzio's. And the swish of his clothes was Iuzio's.

This is how foolish your grandmother really was, Chi.

'Take care, Horki, take care,' my nugget continued to whisper. 'Remember what Iuzio told you.'

But my desire to be with my ancestor was much too strong.

The man stopped pacing.

'And what do you see when you look into your nugget of gold?' he asked suddenly.

I had to think for a while about this.

'Well,' I finally answered, laughing a little. 'Sometimes I'm looking and don't know what I'm supposed to be looking for.'

I didn't know if I'd given him the right answer, but I wanted to please him. I had come to love Iuzio so much.

'And what do you see when you look now, Horki?' he asked.

I brought the nugget up to my face and looked, but I couldn't see a thing in the darkness and wanted to take the nugget outside so that I could properly answer his question.

'No, Horki,' he said, stopping me. 'It's important

to learn to see yourself in darkness, so that you can protect yourself. After all, if you can see yourself in the darkness, imagine how much more easily you'll be able to see yourself in the light.'

I went back to my father's wise words: 'The darkness conceals the light. There is light in the darkness.' And I thought this was a test that Iuzio was giving me, a test to find light in darkness. Realising this made me feel grown up and proud.

So I began to think that this man was making a lot of sense and I saw no reason to mistrust him. I tried looking into my nugget again, but it was frustrating because I couldn't see anything at all. And he came to join me, to help me, he said, as he looked over my shoulder at the nugget. He put his hand over my hand and his hand felt cool, very different from the warm cheek I had kissed all those years ago.

And then I suddenly saw myself in the nugget's surface. It was as if a flare had suddenly been lit and was illuminating my reflection. I was beautiful. My eyes were like two soft dark alluring pools, my cheeks were indented like the cheeks of a woman and my lips were full and parted and the most perfect shape. I had never seen such beauty upon a face before.

'Didn't I tell you that you would be able to see yourself in the darkness, Horki?' the man said excitedly.

'Iuzio, I'm beautiful! I'm so beautiful!' I sang.

'Of course you are,' he came back to me. 'And imagine now how beautiful you are going to look in the light. There is much more for you to discover, Horki. Remember that such beauty is worthy of earning many more nuggets of gold like this one and of attracting the most handsome men from lands far and wide.'

'Is this true?' I was saying excitedly. 'Is this really true? Is my face really so beautiful?'

He laughed again and held his hand over mine. When he took it away, the image of beauty faded and the nugget became dark again.

'Which would you choose, Horki?' he said, his voice echoing in the cave. 'Would you prefer to see yourself in the darkness so that you can see yourself in the light? Or would you prefer not to see yourself at all?'

I thought about this as he gently took the nugget out of my hand. He began examining it closely, twisting and turning it as if he had never seen a nugget of gold before.

Then he closed his fist around it.

'I think I had better keep this for you for a while,' he said. 'It will need to be kept safe. I will polish it for you, so that you will see you are even more beautiful than before. Your beauty will astound everyone, Horki. Everyone.'

It all sounded so exciting, but I didn't quite understand.

'So I don't need to polish the nugget for myself then?' I asked him. 'That's what you said before.'

'I sometimes say things I don't mean,' he replied.

And that was when I first started to doubt, Chi. A small realisation that he wasn't who he appeared to be shot through me. But the memory of my beautiful face was strong enough to keep me there, in his power. I wanted that beautiful face more than anything in the world. I wanted wealth, I wanted handsome men to court me, I wanted whatever the nugget could bring me.

'Let us look again,' the man said, putting his hand over mine as we held the nugget together once more.

And this time in the nugget's reflection I saw myself reclining on an exotic bed, being wooed by princes. I saw myself draped in the most extravagant silken veils, bathed and pampered by slave girls and boys who were keen to serve my every need. I saw great white palaces and domed temples where I was worshipped, and kings from faraway lands coming to honour me.

I couldn't believe how real all of this looked.

The man promised me that all this would one day be mine if only I would allow him to take my nugget into his care. He promised me that he would be faithful to me. And

39

he walked up and down, up and down, holding the nugget in his hand, telling me that this was my one and only chance to accept my true destiny and the gift of supreme beauty, which would remain unchanged forever.

'Forever?' I asked excitedly. 'I will be beautiful forever?'

'Yes, Horki.'

'And I will never grow old?'

'No, Horki. That would be my gift to you if you were to give the nugget of gold to me. Think about it. Should you deny yourself your true destiny?'

It sounded so enticing, but again my doubts returned. I didn't want to have doubts. I wanted to lie on silken cushions, dripping with wealth and power. I wanted to be entertained by princes and kings. But either Iuzio had changed or this was not Iuzio at all. I was suddenly filled with horror and instinctively took a step away from the man in front of me.

And when he turned around I knew for certain that this was not Iuzio, that this was not the man I had met as a child. And at last I was acknowledging that.

He was playing the game of Akahna, wasn't he? And I might already have become a halfwit.

'What is the matter with you, Horki?' he was asking, holding the nugget to his bloated lips as if he was about to eat it. Yes, I could see his lips clearly by this time, and his large black eyes, bulging out of his forehead.

How could I have confused him with Iuzio?

I could see how much those large lips wanted to curl themselves around my little nugget as he began licking it with the longest tongue I had ever seen.

'Nothing,' I muttered, trembling, trying to disguise the fear that was now in my voice.

I wanted to ask for my nugget back, but I couldn't get the words out of my mouth. My throat was constricting; my spirit had frozen.

Then the man started tossing the nugget in the air. Higher and higher it went, so that I thought it might hit the

40

cave ceiling. I was certain he suspended it in the air, just to demonstrate what strange magic he was able to perform.

'Don't you want me to polish this nugget for you, child?' he was asking, with what now seemed to be sarcasm. He was pacing up and down again. 'I'd do it very well, Horki. Remember what I said – if you never get to see yourself in darkness, how are you ever going to see yourself in light? And there will be all that captivating beauty going to waste. A terrible shame, Horki. A terrible, terrible shame.'

I didn't know how to answer that. The trouble was, what he said about darkness and light made sense to me.

'If you say no to this offer, child,' he went on, 'you may just live to regret your decision. You'll grow old, irreversibly old, so very quickly. That isn't what you want – is it?'

My heart was racing. I didn't know what to say or do. I could see the man very clearly by now. His eyes and hair were as black as the night. I was sure that if he were to grin I would see very large white teeth. He was nothing like Iuzio at all. How could I have been so mistaken? How could I have been so stupid?

Who was he?

'You're not Iuzio, are you?' My throat was hot and dry as the words fell out of my mouth.

He laughed a deep throaty laugh, and then he opened his mouth wide so that it became as big as the grinning cave. And then I saw his teeth, large and white. And he laughed and laughed quite as if he had wanted to laugh at me for a very long time.

Was this what people did when you put your trust in them?

He opened his hands, his great ugly palms outstretched towards me, showing me that the nugget had gone. This was trickery. This was magic. It was hard to believe I had fallen into such a trap.

Could this be a dream? My head was spinning. I was sweating and shivering at the same time. Could I pinch myself to wake myself up?

The man opened his mouth slowly, so slowly. And then I saw my little nugget dropping down through the air from the ceiling, where he must have been keeping it all this time. And slowly it disappeared into his mouth.

And there was nothing I could do about it.

He had swallowed the nugget whole. And now he was looking at me and smiling and licking his lips as though he had just eaten something nice.

And I thought, 'Who could swallow a nugget of gold whole like that? What human being could do such a thing?'

No human being could do such a thing! I ran out of the cave in terror. 'Iuzio, what have I done?' I was crying. 'You entrusted me with this little piece of gold and somebody – or something – just ate it!'

I could hear him laughing behind me.

By the time I reached the outside world, I knew this man, this spirit, this shadow, whatever he was, had gone. I sensed that he had perhaps slipped back into the darkest pockets of the Shadow Lands, where he would be squatting in some corner, savouring the luxurious taste of gold.

I imagined the droplet going down, whole, inside him, like a rodent passing whole along the body of a snake. And weakened and depressed, I curled up outside the cave for the night, not minding if wolves or snakes ate me, not minding if bandits carried me away. I curled myself up very tight. I wanted to wake from this dream I was in. I heard my people calling me home. But I couldn't go back to the camp until the dream had ended, until my little nugget of gold was safely back in the palm of my hand once again.

* * * * *

Does gold taste luxurious? Yes, Chi, it does. It was said in an earlier time that people would start eating copper, silver and gold, and once the very first grain of a precious metal had passed their lips their fate would be sealed and they would never stop eating. As I have said, if humans fall madly in love with something, they will want to devour it.

Yes, it is something that can happen very easily, Chi.

So I had been entertained in the cave by a dark shadow, a man who was not a man, a man who was only an illusion.

I woke in darkness, sweating and shivering still. I had never been away from my people at night before. I had never been alone in the darkness before; I'd always had siblings sleeping around me back at the camp. Remember that I was just thirteen at this time, Chi, far too young to be experiencing such things alone, but old enough to understand the messages that were coming to me loud and clear.

Was I still dreaming? Yes, I thought I was. There was an otherworldly feel to everything outside the cave. The ground felt unsafe, a wolf howled, a frog croaked, the moon was full to the east and the breeze was blowing in from that place we had become so mistrustful of. I was now realising that all these omens were unfavourable and having ignored so many warnings, I was going to have to take far more care.

Chi, let me tell you that there can be a dreamer where there is no dream, and a dream where there is no dreamer. Beware the dream that has no dreamer. For the dream develops a life of its own. It wanders aimlessly across the landscape looking for a dreamer foolish enough to entertain it. Trust me when I say that should something of your soul attach itself to such a dream, you may find yourself eternally floating, and it will not be a very pleasant sensation, especially when you realise what is happening. That is what is meant when our people say that you can become lost in a dream. It is probably more appropriate to say that you can become *chained* to a dream.

Was I the dreamer or the dream? I had lost my gold nugget, the thing I treasured most, the thing that had given me so many warnings that I had chosen to ignore. And my lack of respect might now have subjected me to its wrath.

So my guess was that a dream had well and truly chained itself to my soul.

The full moon in the east with her bright stars and the wind in the south with his cold ugly sighs were conspiring against me. Many shadows were beginning to dance. The world of substance was beginning to fade.

Outside the cave I saw my own shadow coming to life in the moonlight. Seeming to form from the moonlight itself, it began to walk about independently.

This was shocking to me.

Yet let me tell you that my shadow was extremely beautiful. She looked exactly like me, but was sophisticated, lithe and carefree as she moved about in extravagant colourful misty veils. Any girl would envy her beauty; any man would throw himself at her feet.

I watched this shadow place a nugget of gold in her mouth, savouring the taste as she chewed it round and round before swallowing it whole, all the while expressing the greatest pleasure.

I instinctively knew that now she would want to eat equally powerful things, such as animals and birds and humans, and perhaps even rocks, trees, castles and the very air we breathe. (Yes, Chi, shadows can even eat the air.) But gold would continue to be a delicacy, I could tell.

I knew I was seeing what I could become in the future should my hunger for gold run out of control.

And even though it scared me, oh Chi, how I yearned for it.

I remained crouched behind a rock for a very long time. And I started to believe that I might just have encountered Beng himself in the cave.

And could I hear the croaking of a frog?

Yes, Chi, Beng is a master of transformation and will disguise himself as a frog or a toad, because in the guise of a frog he is in his most dangerous form. Know that you can touch Beng and he will instantly turn into something you desire, Chi. He can become a prince or princess, or anyone you would dearly love to have standing beside you.

44

But once you have succumbed, you are gobbled up alive. For Beng doesn't grant you a wish without eating you at the same time. He has such an enormous appetite. Yes, this dangerous magical art of his is all about devouring and nothing will be too large or too small for him to eat. He will even eat many things up all at the same time.

It has been said that Beng can stand in the flames of a fire and not get burnt, and that he can seal himself in ice and not freeze. If he masquerades as your mother, your father, your sister, your husband, your lover, your child, you might never know that it is him sitting beside you. One of our people, it was said, had lived with his family for a whole year before learning that Beng had masqueraded as each one of them, all at the same time. And it took a further nine moons, they said, for the tribe's holy man to bring the souls of each person back to the living world again.

Sometimes this is more likely to take nine years.

So you must be wary of shapes that change from one thing to another in an instant, for such an enchantment will render you senseless. You will become a halfwit and there will be no turning back. But my mother told me that we will be safe as long as we remember the origins of things – and as long as we remain wary of frogs.

I knew that Beng would have had no difficulty in pretending to be Iuzio in the cave. So now I was desperately trying to rid myself of the image of Par, the man I was destined to marry. Par was a very wise and handsome young man, a man who put self-worth before power, a man who understood real beauty and the spirit of gold, a man who knew about frogs. Par would never want to gobble me up alive – except in fun. So, in my mind, I was deliberately changing Par into someone I loathed, someone not unlike the slobbering old man in the market-place, so that Beng would not be tempted to change into my beloved man and lure me to my doom.

Some say that Beng was once human, or that a small part of him was – no one really knows which part. Others say he is a spirit of otherworldly making and that there is nothing human about him at all. But now every bit of him is soul-less. Now he is such a master of illusion that he can even look back at you from your own reflection in the river and you can well believe that he is you.

Oh yes.

My people have said that if everyone in the world were to resist Beng, there would be no more souls for him to eat and he would eventually die of starvation. But they have also said that that day is a long way off. For, strangely, so many do not mind being eaten, and even go seeking it. And more and more people might well find such a thing attractive in the future, although none of us know why.

So it works in this way, Chi: a bad spirit eats a soul, regurgitates it and passes it over to Beng, its master. And the more bad spirits or shadows there are, the more food there is likely to be for their master. Because as soon as you have been eaten by him, you will become a shadow yourself and are thereafter gifted with his hunting skills. And his shadows believe that they are always getting a good meal, but they are not in fact getting anything at all, because everything is regurgitated and made ready for their lord and master. And that is why they are eternally hungry and never find satisfaction.

So many shadows. So many shadows. No one can tell how many shadows there will be on earth in the future. There will be many, Chi.

I lay curled against the rock and my thoughts and questions kept coming. How would I know when Beng was in my presence? How would I know that Iuzio wasn't Beng and Beng wasn't Iuzio? Would I ever be able to tell the difference between them? Would I ever know what was real and what wasn't?

I held onto the words Iuzio had spoken to me as a child. I closed my eyes tight in the cold night air and spoke the words loudly, firmly, quickly, all in one breath, to make a spell for myself:

'You must keep looking into the nugget until you see yourself as you truly are, because a lesson is going to

come to you about the temptations of gold and what is going to happen in the future and you must remember when you look at yourself in the River of Life that the water is a clever mistress and her deception runs deep.'

I caught my breath afterwards, hoping that these quickly spoken words might create some powerful magic for me. I left them hanging in the moonlit air, adorning the night sky around me like pieces of glittering gold and silver hanging on a dark bride. I knew that if I could fill the air with my passion to survive I might be able to change my luck.

I could see luzio in my mind's eye, sitting beside his fire, as I had seen him all those years ago. I reasoned that all stars knew the wind. And if I said the words loudly enough, my spell would become airborne and by the power of the spirit of the wind would be transported to the stars, and to luzio himself, who would hear his own words and come to help me.

I lay resting as best I could and slipped off to sleep. But then I woke with a start, feeling something moving about upon me – a firm warm weight upon my chest and stomach. At first I accepted it, as we do living out in the wild where small animals are likely to crawl upon us for comfort or warmth. But as I roused myself I became aware that this was a frog, large and dark, looking at me with great yellow eyes.

It was Beng, appearing to me in his most natural guise. And before he had chance to change into something I desired or feared, I closed my eyes and screamed: 'You are a frog! You are a frog! You are a frog!'

I screamed the words three times, then seven times, then nine times, to give them the greatest power. Then I leapt in the air, knocking the frog off me, letting him know that I was not going to take his nonsense.

But something quietened me: a woman's voice.

Yes, Chi, a woman was suddenly speaking to me in the otherworldly air.

'Quick! Quick!' I heard her saying. 'Over here!

Come, come, child, if you know what is good for you.'

I looked about for the source of the voice and saw, just above the cave, the outline of a woman waving at me from within the foliage of the cave's hair. I could just about make out her shape in the moonlight. It was comforting to hear a woman speaking to me. But was she real, appearing so suddenly like this? Was this another of Beng's disguises?

I stepped towards her cautiously, as she held out her hand.

'You must come away from this place,' she told me. 'There is little time. Come, come quickly now.'

I didn't recognise her as one of our own people, though her dark looks told me she was an Egyptian.

'Who are you?' I asked.

'Don't waste time,' she called urgently. 'You *must* come quickly. I will explain things later.'

At that point a great and ferocious wind started to blow, which told me that Beng might be coming back to get me. It was said that winds blew unexpectedly when strong magic was in the air. So I took the woman's hand, allowing her to steer me through the foliage hair and into a tent in which a warm fire was burning, the smoke passing up through a hole in the roof.

The tent was elegant. I had never stood in anything quite so elegant before. And this led me to assume that the woman was a member of one of the more wealthy nomadic tribes who travelled constantly from east to west and from west to east, trading and gathering riches as they went. She might have been a queen or a princess, judging by the soft, shiny, extravagant cloth that decorated the inside of the tent and by the comfortable cushions. And she herself merged beautifully and dreamily with the tent. I began to wonder if I was in the presence of the spirit of the moon herself.

Perhaps I was still enchanted. But I saw no cause to panic. I considered it easier to escape from a woman. So I decided I would give her the opportunity to prove herself. I so badly needed to trust someone.

She had soon wrapped a bright soft blanket around me, rubbing my arms because I had become so cold. And then she filled a beaker from a small cauldron above the fire and gave me delicious wine to warm me. Was I also drinking this comforting silvery light? By this time I didn't care. I drank and rested and grew tired.

And then I asked her: 'Who are you? Are you Lady Shon, the spirit of the moon?'

And: 'Can I trust you?'

'Sssh, little one,' she said, holding me and rocking me and laughing at the same time.

'But can I trust you?'

'If you look at what I have to show you,' she told me, 'you can decide for yourself. I am going to help you understand all that has been happening to you in this place. Your destiny has been carved out for you, Horki. You are on earth for a purpose. You have been chosen for a special task, which involves helping your people. You have been born with a great gift which needs to be nurtured.'

'Gift? I have a gift?'

She smiled. 'Yes, Horki, many of your people do. And certainly you do.'

I saw no strange darkness in her eyes or anywhere within the tent. She did not have big teeth, but was warm, caring and kind. And most importantly, she was talking sense. I knew that my people carried special knowledge and had clever ways, which many envied. But she was also confirming something I had long thought to be true: that I was special.

I was beginning to trust her.

'Me? Special?' I mumbled to myself. 'Me? With a gift? So it is really true after all.'

I knew then that I had been destined to step into this tent at this particular time so that I could have all of this confirmed to me.

I pulled the blanket more closely around me. I gulped the wine. I was trembling from head to toe, excited by what was to happen in the future.

But then I wanted to know what she thought about the disappearance of my gold nugget.

'A man stole my nugget,' I told her with a pout.

I meant to say more, but couldn't finish. The strong wine was making me feel drowsy. Yet I was certain deep down that this was all compensation for all the pain and suffering I'd been through in the cave with Beng. And the woman confirmed this as she said reassuringly, 'We are all brought to trials and tests before we earn the right to merge with our true destiny, Horki.'

I understood. I knew that Beng had provided the test she spoke of. And now this beautiful lady was bringing me my prize.

I was desperate to know her name.

'You may call me Dai,' she said, her arm about me as she began stroking my hair. 'I would like to think that I was a mother to you. Know that you are safe now. One who is endowed with such a gift as you have needs special protection at all times. These are dangerous times, as you have already discovered.'

Her hand seemed to be made of pure warm light as it moved a strand of hair away from my face, tucking it behind my ear in a motherly way.

This woman was everything I wanted her to be.

'Are you a queen?' I asked her, my voice a little slow. 'Have I entered a dream?'

'Sssh!' she said again, rocking me, her face against mine. 'Drink your wine. And remember that queens and dreams are one, my child. You will come to understand such wisdom soon. Rest, for now you are come home.'

Yes, I was come home. 'I am come home,' I repeated, slurring, as we rocked together.

She tucked another strand of hair behind my ear with an ethereal hand.

'What is my gift?' I had to ask. 'Are you going to tell me what my gift is to be?'

She pulled herself back and looked at me with surprise. 'Don't you know, child?' she asked.

50

I shook my head. 'I know it is something special,' I said, 'but I know nothing more. I would so love to know what it will be. What am I destined for? Do tell me, Dai. Tell me.'

She pulled herself away so that she could take my face in both her hands. 'Do you think you would like to glimpse the future then?'

'Oh, yes. Yes, please! Show me. Show me now!'

'Let us look together then,' she said. And she produced a large crystal ball which she placed between us. It was perfectly round and as soon as I looked into it I saw many colours and milky white patterns, all swimming about together.

'Watch the colours and the patterns,' Dai said. 'Keep looking at them, little one, and as they clear you will start to see your future.'

As I watched the beautiful colours I felt a great desire inside, a great yearning to belong to this strange new adult world I was experiencing. I wanted to see and know *everything*. And as the colours swirled and grew brighter, so my yearning churned and grew stronger. I felt a hunger for knowledge that I had never known before. It cut deep down inside me, like a bolt of lightning, pushing something up out of me like fire. Yes, the hunger of fire, like urgent flames, passionately and tirelessly licking logs, was rising up in me. And the feeling was so strong that I was sure it was lighting me up from inside.

And then the colours parted at their centre and as they began spreading out I saw sparkling rivers winding away into the distance, and jewels winking within them, and all of it under the clearest bluest sky.

'It is beautiful,' I said, drooling.

'Keep looking, keep looking,' Dai urged.

I did, and soon saw a small figure moving along. The figure was difficult to see at first, but then she became larger and brighter. And then I knew that it was me.

I was riding upon something – no, I was being carried on a great colourful silken-veiled litter. I was dressed in the most magnificent gold robe, which was so bright that I couldn't look upon it without squinting. The robe's light stretched for miles around, making me every bit as bright as Kam, the spirit of the sun, himself.

Four men were carrying me, and my entourage, numbering hundreds, was stretching way before me and way behind. These were handpicked people who were serving the royal household, from counsellors and priests down to soldiers and slaves. Numerous mules, camels, horses and elephants were also travelling with us, bearing our magnificent cargo.

'Is that me?' I asked, even though I knew that it was.

'Yes, that is you, little one,' Dai replied, her arm about me, occasionally giving my shoulder a reassuring squeeze.

'Where is this caravan going?'

'You are going to a distant land, child, where you are to become queen.'

'Which land?' I asked, thrilled. I wanted to know if we were travelling west, if we would be crossing a great water.

She answered immediately. 'You will travel across many waters, across many mountains, plains, deserts and valleys. You are seeing the land of the future, my child.'

I didn't understand this, but she told me to keep watching and I would find my answers.

I saw the train winding its way across a vast landscape, over magnificent rocks and cliffs, along vast plains and deserts, down into deep valleys and gorges and up into the tallest ranges of mountains. It did not tire for one moment. It just wove on and on, with people paying homage along the way and gifts being laid before me.

Whenever we paused to make camp, I was carefully lowered to the ground and people came from far and wide to hear me speak of my people and our ancient ways, and how these ways were fast slipping away.

But was I really talking about our ancient ways?

I questioned the woman about this, for she was still looking into the crystal.

'Watch,' was all she said.

And as I returned my eyes to the crystal I soon realised that I wasn't, in fact, talking about our ancient ways at all. I was talking about the future, which seemed to be much more important than the present or the past.

I was telling people of the Golden City to which I was travelling, a magnificent town nestled upon one of the tallest mountains in the world. This was a place where giant golden-crested temples rose up into the sky, where roads, paved honey gold, wove in and out of the landscape, where the very fabric of the dwellings was polished with the essence of the sun and where no one wanted for anything, because they had everything they were ever going to need.

This had to be paradise.

And it was in this city that I would be crowned queen, chosen for my beauty and wealth, chosen above all others because the great gift I was carrying within me could only ever come alive in this one place.

And there, at the heart of it all, would be the most handsome king anyone had ever seen, and he was destined to become my husband.

I thought that he might be Kam, the spirit of the sun, himself.

This was thrilling to me, but I couldn't believe that I was destined for this. I didn't know if I deserved it. But oh, Chi, that feeling, that surge of hunger, that bolt of lightning – it was there again.

I looked into the crystal for more, and saw princes and princesses, great men of learning and men and women of extraordinary wealth all bowing before me, all clamouring to win a place in my heart and in my entourage, because all of them desired more than anything the chance to earn citizenship in the Golden City. It seemed that everyone was wanting to live in this most distinguished land. One after another they came, as I sat on my golden throne in my great silken tent, each one begging me for citizenship. My passage was assured; theirs was uncertain. And so they offered all they had to impress me and secure their future.

As I partook of fruit, a strange golden fruit picked from a special golden tree which was being carried in a great golden casket by a golden-clad elephant, these people offered me gifts: silks, satins, spices, animals, their allegiance, some of them their very souls. My toes tickled from the many kisses they received. These people would do anything for me, so desperate were they to reach the Golden City.

I was kind to them. I didn't have to be. I could have turned them all away, left them all wandering alone in the heat of the desert. I could have had any number of them slaughtered.

Instead I dipped my hand into a large casket of golden coins, small tokens which ran through my fingers, tinkling down onto a mound of others below, tempting the people in front of me, tormenting them. These trinkets had been minted behind the gates of the great Golden City, I told them. And they could be theirs, in abundance, if they proved themselves worthy.

I knew I could tell them such things, because I knew how important I was. It had reached me that my future husband believed I was the only person in all the world eligible to marry him. I knew this to be true, because there was no one else like me anywhere in the world. People only had to look at me to feel something quaking inside them and to feel the presence of something unutterably powerful touching their souls. And once this power had been linked to the power of my king, it would shake the very foundations of the earth. Together we would make the match that the world had been waiting for for many thousands of years. In the future we would live as one, so that the whole world would be able to live as one. And that would be a wonderful thing. And I saw that the future of the world was secure, Chi.

But there were those who were trying to stop this

future from happening. Their aim was to dissuade me from taking the journey to my beloved lord, and one after another they stepped up to advise me. Harsh words leapt out of their mouths and their limbs flailed about in anger.

Some of them were wielding swords.

These people were jealous. And whenever I observed them closely, I could see that there was no gold upon their persons at all. There was nothing about them that sparkled. These were the people who had no future, and I had no option but to have them cast out, and the more violent ones put to death. But those who wore the tiniest grain of gold upon themselves had hope. For they would be kept under a watchful eye by my priests and soldiers. And they would be nurtured. They were the ones who would find opportunities to succeed.

And so the train wove on, and soon we reached the golden kingdom of my beloved, where people were cheering and welcoming me to my new home.

My king was there to greet us at the great golden gates, waiting on a great rostrum with his own entourage gathered about him. And as I stepped towards him, I saw that he was the most handsome man I had ever seen. The feeling was so special I believed I was stepping up to be kissed by Kam himself.

'Welcome, my queen,' my king said, smiling as he sensuously kissed the palm of my hand.

'My lord,' I returned, curtsying deeply.

As I stepped up onto the great rostrum, I looked out at the many thousands of faces applauding me, bowing to me, desperate to touch me. Soldiers in golden uniforms were brought to the scene to hold the crowds at bay.

When I looked down at my body, I saw that I was not only wearing gold, but my skin was turning the colour of gold. Yes, I was becoming as bright as the sun: pure gold itself. And that alone seemed to be driving the crowd wild.

And I found it hard to look upon my king for any length of time, because he dazzled me with his golden beauty. His skin too being golden, it was as though he were fashioned out of sunlight itself.

And that feeling, that surge, was there again, that hunger, that bolt of lightning which I was now beginning to enjoy. The passion within me was becoming almost painful, but at the same time ecstatic. And I knew that only here in this place could this great hunger be truly satisfied.

Yes, as Dai had said, I had come home.

'What my new queen has will benefit us all,' the king then announced to his people, *our* people, his honeyed voice echoing about the great courtyards of this remarkable city. 'She is about to give to me what I have been waiting for for such a long time. And for that I am truly grateful.'

He kissed my knuckles again and again.

And then our lips met, and everyone clapped and cheered, as we came together, embracing in a magnificent golden dance that would last for an eternity and which everyone would celebrate forever more.

My love and I, and our people, within our city, were at last one.

And then I grew very tired, but pleasantly so. The crystal ball and the wine were causing my eyelids to droop. But I didn't mind. I was happy, so happy that the future was now secured.

Dai tucked me up. I loved her so much. And I slipped easily and peacefully off to sleep.

But remember, Chi, remember that you can fall asleep within a dream.

And sometimes that can be your undoing, for that is when you are in danger of becoming hopelessly enchanted.

And that may easily have happened to me, but for the fact that I woke with a sadness in my soul, a soft sadness that had replaced the intense thirst. And suddenly I wondered if I had been tricked.

Dai was still close beside me, sometimes singing in my ear, and although her voice soothed me, it seemed half-hearted. She was running her fingers through my hair, but her touch was uncertain. She had a look of doubt in her eye.

I wanted her to be as she had been. I wanted her to

be sure about my future. I wanted to have no more worry, pain or fear, no more responsibility or concern. I wanted the infinite childhood dressed in stars, where little girls only dream of being women, and I wanted that opportunity to have whatever I wanted, whenever I wanted it.

I wanted it *all*, because I was Horki, and because Horki was special, and because Horki had a gift.

And Chi, it wasn't a real sleep I had fallen into but a great blissful enchantment, a dish of pure sweet honey. Drifting on a sea of sugar and sensual pleasure and passion, I was gloriously lost within an illusion.

And so you would be if you had just met Ana, the wife of Beng.

* * * * *

Remember, Chi, that both Beng and Ana will be out to beguile you, Beng with his mysterious darkness, Ana with her adorning light. Both will be out to work their magic on you.

I had been feeling too good, meaning that my guard had been down. And before I knew it, Ana might have swallowed me whole and regurgitated me for her husband to eat, as that is what Ana is so good at doing.

But she didn't. Why didn't she? Hadn't she lured and won me for her lord and master? Hadn't she played her part in the great sorcerer's bargain?

At the time I didn't understand that I had met her. And if I did not understand her badness, I understood her sadness even less.

But I expect you will be wondering how I escaped from Ana, and whether I retrieved my nugget of gold.

Well, when I looked outside Ana's tent I realised why I had heard her voice echoing whenever she had been laughing or singing. We had been in the cave for the whole of the time, though she had blinded me into thinking we were somewhere very different. And I ran outside to find the moon full in the east and the stars in the same position

57

as they had been before, and I realised that no time had actually passed at all.

Time will stand still, Chi, when your soul is about to be eaten.

As Iuzio has said, 'When you become enchanted by Beng, the past, present, future and experience become so entangled and inseparable that they merge into one and you no longer know which is which. You are being given a false sense of immortality, an immortality built entirely of shadow.'

As soon as I realised that I had been entertained by Ana, I looked back into the cave and discovered that there was actually nothing there: no tent and no evidence that anyone had ever been there.

I was confused, saddened and disappointed all at the same time. The Golden City had seemed such a wonderful place.

Would there ever be anyone I could trust again?

* * * * *

Perhaps I was foolish for thinking I did not want to leave without my nugget of gold. But I found myself looking around for a weapon, a big stick, so that I could return to the cave and demand it back.

And during my search for the stick I came across a waterhole and caught my reflection looking back at me from the moonlit water. As I looked at my face, swimming about, Iuzio's words came rushing back, words about looking for myself and about the illusions that are contained within reflections.

I brought my face very close to the water's surface, so that my nose was almost touching it, and my reflection darkened as I heard our beloved ancestor's words once again: 'A lesson is going to come to you, Horki.'

As I moved back a little from the water I was able to see myself more clearly, even though the moonlight was pale and the breeze was disturbing the water. I pulled faces at myself, as children do, and then I imagined diving deep down into my own reflection, down and down and down into the many depths that abound below the surface. And I remembered my elders telling me that to dive into one's own reflection was to dive into one's own soul, where one would find the wings of liberation or the chains of doom. Water, they said, had the power to stir every single memory that was within you.

I knew my elders practised this diving art, but I didn't know if I should be doing it at this time. So I moved away from the waterhole. And as I turned, I was startled by a figure standing directly behind me, the darkened figure of a man.

After jumping with fright I found strength I never knew I possessed. I quickly broke a branch off a nearby bush and held it up to the man who was slowly advancing towards me.

'I will strike you,' I warned, determined that I was not going to be fooled a third time. 'Believe me, I will strike you, spirit. I swear I will strike you if you step any closer.'

As my eyes adjusted to the darkness I began to see his shape a little more clearly. He looked like Iuzio. But I was more than ready now for tricks.

'Who are you?' I demanded loudly, still nervously clutching the stick. 'Which one are you? Answer me.'

'Which one do you want?' came the very calm reply.

'Don't play games with me!' I cried, tightening my grip on the stick. 'I will use this if I have to! I've had enough!'

'Good,' he said, smiling, tossing his brown shawl over his shoulder in a relaxed manner and putting his hands into the sleeves of his robe. He held his head to one side as he observed me.

'I'm glad,' he said, nodding to himself. 'I've been waiting to hear you say that.'

His words threw me. Here I was, holding a stick high

in the air ready to strike him, and there he was praising me for it. Was this the real Iuzio? I was prepared to fight him if he wasn't. Maybe I was prepared to fight him if he was.

I watched him carefully as he sat down on a rock. He was doing everything so very calmly and slowly. Or perhaps I was just moving too fast.

'You want to retrieve the nugget of gold I gave you, Horki,' he said, folding his legs, his hands still in his sleeves. 'But you will need to decide which nugget you want.'

This confused me and my arms slackened a little as I frowned.

He continued: 'Do you desire real gold? Or that which looks like gold?'

I thought about this. There was only one nugget of gold, wasn't there? The nugget which also happened to look like gold. As far as I knew they were one and the same object.

As I put this to him, the moon scudded out from behind a cloud and it was then that I clearly saw his red hair and blue eyes, along with the smile that I remembered from all those years ago. I was sure then that this was the real Iuzio.

'Do not be deceived by gold, Horki,' he continued. 'Gold is like water. And both gold and water will deceive you if you look into either of them and refuse to see yourself as you are. A great lesson came to you about gold when you were advised by the spirit in the cave to look for yourself in the darkness so that you could more easily see yourself in the light. Did you believe this to be good advice?'

I didn't answer. I didn't know how to answer. His wisdom was beyond me. But I was ashamed, because the words had made so much sense to me at the time.

He explained: 'Do not look for yourself within the darkness, Horki, but for the darkness within yourself. Do not look for yourself within the light, but for the light within yourself. And never look for yourself within the One, but for the one within yourself. It is up to each one of us to learn such things.'

60

I was staring at him. I didn't know if I wanted such choices.

Iuzio was giving me that wistful smile of amusement that I remembered so well. And I knew that he knew what I was thinking.

'I understand,' he said simply.

Then: 'Wouldn't you like to put that stick down now?'

I finally lowered the stick to the ground, blushing with embarrassment.

And it was then that he told me that I had been entertained not by a great queen in the tent, but by Ana, wife of Beng.

'But Ana's light felt so comforting and warm and real,' I said. 'It's hard to believe that there was nothing there at all in that cave, that it was all just an illusion.'

'It is a hard lesson, Horki, isn't it? The beauty of gold deceives us, as it will deceive a great many in the future.'

'I never thought the spirit of gold was capable of deceiving me,' I mumbled, moodily. 'And I never thought a woman as beautiful and as caring as Ana was capable of deceiving me either.'

'Everything on earth is capable of deception, Horki. But the greatest deceiver will usually be yourself.'

I moved forward so that I could look at Iuzio more closely. I wanted to look at his red hair and blue eyes again. Was I still in the dream? Whose dream was this? Mine or his?

'Look for the dream within yourself, Horki, not the dream within others,' I heard myself saying.

I began to feel my blood coming back, pulsing in my veins. Looking down at my hands I vividly remembered them being bright gold and now observed that they were, thankfully, made of flesh once again.

'You must take care now, Horki,' Iuzio told me. 'Beng's Locollico spirits know when mortals are young and beginning to grow. And they will seek out those who are vulnerable, and when they have found you, they will do all they can to familiarise you with their ways. They need to catch you before you have time to learn what the worlds of shadow and substance are all about. In the future, people are destined to remain at this vulnerable stage of life for a long time. A delay in maturity will halt their rite of passage. So those who reach thirty years may still be just thirteen. And those who reach fifty years may still be just fifteen. People will be looking for themselves within their age rather than their age within themselves, Horki.'

I thought I understood. 'Is this Beng's work?'

'Yes, this is the One's work.'

Beng was often referred to as 'the One'. And I rarely heard Iuzio speak of him in any other way.

'You believe you met the One in the cave, don't you?' he told me.

'Didn't I?'

'No, Horki. You met one of his Locollico spirits, one of his children. Only when the One is about to eat you will you properly see him in person. He designs it that way because he wishes to keep his identity secret. You must remember that those who encounter the One rarely live to tell the tale. No one who has been eaten by him, or who has come anywhere close to that, has ever returned to describe his true form.'

'Because they have lost their memories, and their eyes and ears?'

'Yes, Horki.'

'But Ana must have seen him,' I said, 'because she is his wife and lives with him. He has never eaten her.'

'He has never eaten her because she was once a woodland queen. She is still remembered in the most ancient of forests,' Iuzio answered. 'But Ana remains loyal to her lord and master, so foolishly loyal, and will never reveal his secrets. She is much too afraid of him to do that.'

Iuzio seemed reflective as he spoke these words. And as young as I was, I knew that he had experienced far more of Beng and Ana's liaison than he was prepared to divulge to me.

'So you have never yet met Beng,' I said, 'otherwise you wouldn't be here. You would be in his belly.'

Iuzio laughed. 'Perhaps,' he said, 'but it would be very difficult for the One to eat me because I am immortal. Still, Horki, I may yet find myself in such a position in the future, should fate throw us together.'

I reflected on this, recalling too how my people said that Beng could only perish if starved out of existence. No more halfwits meant no more food.

'I am so glad that the Locollico spirit didn't eat me,' I told Iuzio.

'So am I, Horki. Ana would certainly have eaten you too had it not been for your sadness.'

'My sadness?'

'It was when you fell asleep that you would have been eaten. You had drunk from Ana's beaker. It was the beaker rather than the wine that enchanted you. But your sadness affected Ana, causing her to reflect with her own inner water. Remember that reflection disturbs both the One and his queen. True feeling will cause Ana to become doubtful and the One to simply slink away. Water is therefore a good defence. It will protect all mortals from harm. Remember that no bad spirit will ever touch you, Horki, if you allow water to enter your soul.'

'Poor Ana. I feel sorry for her,' I said.

Iuzio took my hand. 'Of course, Horki. But we can afford to have hope for her. She still carries a lot of her ancient magic. That is why the One took her for a wife, rather than for a meal. Ana is ashamed of herself. And sometimes when you hear the wind moaning in the mountains at night, it is not the wind but Ana's sad voice, crying for her loyal woodland people and for what used to be and for what she has done to herself. You helped her to feel a little sadness again in that cave, Horki. And how else will we remind her of what she once had, of the old life in the woodland and of her loyal people?

'Unfortunately, her hunger has become just as great

now as her sadness and she is addicted to winning her master's favour. Her role in the future is uncertain. Even though her immortality prevents her from being eaten, she is still in a terrible situation, doomed to remain shackled to the One forever more, her only hope being that one day she might just outwit the Boro Mulo and escape him. But there are no guarantees that this will ever occur.'

'So she will need to look at her reflection as we all do before she can make any changes?'

'That's right, Horki. But because the One fooled her when she looked at herself a long time ago, she is afraid to look again. He disguised himself as a prince and Ana was deceived.'

'Just as I was deceived by the king in the Golden City,' I said, hanging my head.

'Of course. You were stepping into Ana's own story when you watched yourself in the magic crystal.'

'Poor Ana. But what of the Locollico spirits, Beng's children? Would they need to look at their reflections too to get better?'

'No, Horki. The Locollico were once completely mortal. And mortals need to earn immortality. Mortals who merely assume immortality will have no substance and therefore won't be able to look at their reflections to make themselves whole again. They are doomed to wander the Shadow Lands as dust and shadow forever, all of them held together only by the strings that tie them to the One. Death will be their only release. Death will permit them a greater glimpse of immortality, should they stop to think about it.'

'But if Ana can be helped, you will help her, Iuzio, won't you?' I asked urgently. 'Your magic is strong. You are clever and brave and powerful. And you are a star from up in the sky.'

He was laughing.

'We hope the time will come when we are able to help Ana, Horki. All immortals hope that many things will change in the future.'

I reflected again on my nugget.

'So what about the nugget you gave me? Did the Locollico spirit eat that up instead of me? I wanted to get my nugget back so much because it had become so special to me.'

'You have it back, Horki.'

I frowned.

'Just look within yourself and you'll find it.'

'But it went into the Locollico's mouth. I saw it go.'

'The dark side went into the Locollico's mouth. But that doesn't mean to say he kept it.'

He was looking at me then, waiting for me to say the inevitable.

'I have to look for the gold, the darkness and the light within myself,' I said, with my eyes closed, recalling what I had learned. 'I must not look for myself within any of these things.'

'Not any more,' he confirmed, nodding. 'You are beginning to understand, Horki, which is a difficult thing to do when you are so young. But this is the way it has been for all our people.'

He was still sitting with his legs folded, his head to one side, watching me. And I was so glad he was beside me.

'You are still the real Iuzio,' I announced happily.

'Yes,' he laughed affectionately. 'I am still the real Iuzio. But you were wise to doubt this and to question me, even to threaten me with a stick. Absolute trust is not an Egyptian's way, Horki, and it is by no means a good tool to carry through life. You must never forget that.'

He paused a while to smile at me, amused again, before touching my cheek with his warm fingers.

'Remember that no one can tell you what is real and what isn't, Horki,' he said, as he stroked my cheek. 'It is for each of us to discover this for ourselves.'

I knew then that I loved Iuzio as much as the day I had first met him. And as he had reminded me that I was young, I suddenly wondered how old he was.

'Are you very, very old?' I asked boldly. 'Can you tell me how many grandfathers you are?'

He laughed at me again as he returned his hands to the sleeves of his robe.

'Don't you know that it is impolite to ask this of an ancestor?' he said, lightly scolding me.

He was right. It *was* impolite. My father had made a point of telling all his children that no one should demand personal information from ancestors.

But Iuzio was still smiling. 'How old do you want me to be?' he asked. 'Does the wind tell you how old he is when he comes to cool you in the heat of the desert? Does the rain tell you how old she is when she comes to provide you with water after a drought? You are merely pleased to know that these spirits are there when you need them, Horki.'

This, I was to discover as I grew to know Iuzio better, was how he often answered questions: by giving questions in return. I also learned that the spirits of the wind and the rain, both ageless and timeless, and undoubtedly close friends of his, were not unlike him in many ways. For they too were immortal spirits.

I apologised to Iuzio.

'You will be safe now,' he told me, 'so long as you never forget how close you came to losing your soul. The One and Ana will menace our people for a long time to come, Horki, as they will everyone everywhere who carries knowledge passed down through the generations from the Old Land. And as the cloud of the One's Great Curse slowly steals across the world, growing stronger as each day passes, the effects will be beyond what anyone can imagine.

'It is necessary to understand that the Shadow World is a relentless world with no compromises. Shadows will move across the land unnoticed at first, but soon their forms will solidify until everyone dances to the one tune of the Boro Mulo. And by that time no one will recall what a shadow is, let alone know how to deal with it.

'Remember that the stronger the curse grows, the stronger man's thirst will grow. Many mortals will become the children of Locollico spirits, and more and more children will be regurgitated in the coming centuries, all of them shadows who will attempt to bring the Golden City to earth. You will meet them everywhere, Horki, on street corners and in the most unexpected places.'

He had been holding my hand all the time he had been speaking, and now he looked at me quietly for a few moments before he added, 'If we immortals can do anything to change all this, Horki, know that we will. You and I must do our best not to fail the Long Reflection and our Great Ancestral Chain.'

'What is our Great Ancestral Chain?'

'Seven of you are linked: the seventh in every seven generations stretches back to link with those behind and forward to link with those ahead. You are the first of this seven, Horki, but what the second, third, fourth, fifth and sixth do will be vital in helping me find the seventh person. We have to hope that there will be a seventh in the chain.'

'Supposing there isn't one,' I said, concerned.

'If there isn't one then there can only be one reason: the One will have feasted on that person. He is bent on breaking ancient lines. If he can break ours, he will. Each generation must pass on knowledge and experience in the best way it can, so that we can defeat him.'

'I want there to be a seventh person. I really want this, Iuzio.'

'Then you must learn your lessons well so that you can pass it all down in the old way. Polish your reflection well, Horki, and you will not fail.'

He squeezed my hand.

I understood and swore to him that I would never forget anything he had told me. And I would look at myself every day in the river because I so desperately wanted the reflections of all our people to survive.

'Will I see you again?' I couldn't help asking.

'Of course you will,' he smiled. 'Many times. When you look into the river you will see me. When you look

67

into your children's eyes you will see me. When you look at a sunset or the rising moon you will see me. You will see me in the generations behind you and in the generations ahead of you. Our reflections will keep our spirits strong, Horki.'

'I nearly dived into the water when you came upon me,' I confessed. 'I very nearly dived beyond my reflection, which my father told me I should never do unless I had prepared myself.'

'But you did dive, Horki.'

'I did?'

'Yes. That is how I was able to find you.'

'But I wasn't aware of getting wet.'

He laughed. 'No, because you found the reflection within yourself, not yourself within the reflection. That is what I had been waiting for you to do.'

There was just one more question I had to ask: 'Will our people walk across the blue sheet of silk my father described?'

'Yes,' he said. 'You will go beyond the water, all together, in more ways than one. It isn't far away now. In fact it draws near.'

'When? How near?'

He turned away. I heard him sigh. 'You are curious, little one,' he said, 'but also impatient. I must leave you now because the sun is coming up. There will be many new dawns in the future in which to find your answers. We cannot know everything all at once.'

I wondered then whether I might be dying because he was talking about a new dawn. My father had said that when you died and entered the ancestral realms you saw a new dawn breaking on your horizon, no matter what time of day or night it happened to be. And when I looked to the east, there was a faint golden glow.

Iuzio looked so real, perhaps too real, standing there, now being painted by the new sun's light. Perhaps I was more in his world than in mine.

'Am I dying?' I asked. 'I feel as though I am dying.'

I thought he was going to laugh again, but he lifted

68

my chin and said, 'Something within us is always dying, Horki. Death always comes before life, winter before spring, autumn before winter. So, yes, a part of you is dying now, as it is every day. But a greater part of you will also begin to live every day and you will need to use that part of yourself for the task you have to perform in the future.'

Then he prepared to walk away.

I looked down into my hand and as I did so I saw that the nugget of gold was back in my palm. It was still with me. I closed my fist around it and held it to my heart. And then I threw my arms about Iuzio and kissed him, promising him that I would never let the nugget out of my sight again.

'The nugget has a powerful magic now which will protect you,' he said in my ear as I looked across his shoulder at the oncoming dawn. 'You must go back now, Horki.'

'Back? Where?' I was clinging on to him. I wanted to go with him, or for him to come with me. I didn't mind which. I held his hand to my cheek.

He was laughing at me. 'Horki,' he said, 'you cannot come with me. Not yet. It is not the right time.'

'When, then? When will be the right time? When will I go with you?'

He laughed again. He always seemed to be laughing at me.

'So I am not dying,' I said then, realising. 'I am not dying after all.'

At first that thought saddened me because I so desperately wanted to go with Iuzio. But then I realised that it would be far better not to die, for then I could return to my people and tell them all about him and about what had happened to me. And most importantly, I could carry out my contribution to the seven generations, which would be vital in helping Iuzio and all those in the Great Ancestral Chain to survive.

Reluctantly, I let his hand go.

'I am not dying. I am not dying,' I was saying to

myself. I was proud that I had been able to resist Beng and Ana and their Locollico spirit. I was proud that I had remembered to believe that a frog is a frog.

Then I tried to talk again, but found that I couldn't. I couldn't seem to open my mouth. I couldn't open my eyes either. I felt I was moving through another dream. I was moaning and rolling about.

Then I realised my mother was trying to still me.

'What is she trying to say?' I heard my grandmother asking.

I was lying in our tent on my back. My body was clammy and I was weak. I was trying to thank Iuzio before he went away, but there was so much sweat on my body and I was so uncomfortable that I couldn't get a lucid word beyond my lips.

'She is back,' I heard several voices saying all at once.

'I am back,' I found myself trying to say, but it was garbled.

Outside, the dust was blowing hot and the belly of the tent was smacking in and out in the warm-spirited wind. My father stepped into the tent, bringing a shower of sand with him, along with the strong smell of herbs and spices, the ones he used for people who were sick.

I knew by this time that I had been very ill, perhaps for a long period of time.

I became aware that someone was holding my hand. Par, the young man I was to marry, was beside me, talking to me, although I couldn't hear what he was saying. He was sometimes holding my hand to his cheek. I remembered a night when I had stood with my nugget under the full moon, praying for Par to bond with me. And now here he was desperately praying for my release from the fever.

My nugget is gone, I kept thinking. My nugget is gone. But then I remembered that it was not gone, for it was now safely tucked inside me, not because I had gobbled it up, not because I had swallowed it whole, but because I had chosen to find gold within myself.

70

'She's back,' I heard my mother crying, elated, holding my other hand.

'The fever has passed,' I heard my brother Ag shouting outside.

And then I felt myself being raised up and I knew I was being held in my father's arms and being rocked by him. And I heard my mother and my two sisters weeping beside me, while my father gave thanks to all the spirits for their help.

I kept trying to talk, trying to tell them what was important, but the words were lodged inside me, perhaps held within the gold that I'd just found. The mopping of my brow increased and the smell of the protective spices increased and my father's chants increased. Everyone around me was giving thanks that I had survived.

And only after hearing one word did they all suddenly quieten and grow still around me.

'Iuzio,' I finally mumbled.

And I saw a tear roll down my father's cheek.

* * * * *

That day my father was given the message he had been waiting to hear. He knew that one of his children was destined to meet our beloved ancestor and to pass the memory of our people along the Boro Dikimangro.

My experience remained protected by the gold nugget that was within me and the words I had been longing to speak when I had been emerging from the fever were never spoken. But that is the way of gold and what she teaches us, Chi. You will not be able to recount your experience and shout about it, even though you may wish to. Real experience lives inside you, within that quiet place, and will only make itself known in your actions. That is the effect of the lessons that are given to you by immortal ancestors like the spirit of gold and Iuzio.

And you will doubtless learn all this for yourself, Chi, when you have known the spirit of gold and Iuzio for as long as I have.

I told you once that gold was wonderful to touch, that my nugget was so smooth that I could be touching silk or air. I told you I could hold the nugget to my face and it would caress me, and that I could rub it on my skin and it would heal me. Know, Chi, that I did not lie to you about these things. I see the nugget, smell the nugget, taste the nugget still, because I have discovered its worth within myself, and because I was never tempted to gobble it up greedily after all.

So, when I was thirteen and nearly lost my life, I suddenly found a brand new life. I discovered I had a most important role to play as I went into adulthood. It could have fallen to any one of my nine siblings to bond with Iuzio and to learn the lesson I had learned, but the task fell to me, just as it will fall to you, Chi. You will need to bond with Iuzio too, in your own special way, if you are to form a link in the Great Ancestral Chain.

And now I wonder how the spirit of gold will find her way to you, or whether she will find her way to you at all. For my fear is as great today as it was when Iuzio first uttered those words all those years ago.

Will you be there? I so often see you in the water. Yet still these fears linger.

So, remember the answer to the riddle: *Gold is not gold when it is also copper.*

You must not mistake gold, silver or copper for substitutes, or for power, Chi.

But there is something else.

You see, the riddle fooled our elders.

I was not the only one who was sick with the fever when I was thirteen. I was not the only one who was given a golden nugget. And I was not the only one who visited Beng's cave.

My two sisters, Sonna and Rupe, were also sick and also taken into that cave in their dreams.

My mother had seen a mouse running in and out of our tents when our fevers had been coming on: an omen that Ana was near and conspiring with Beng to distract us from the ancestral inheritance which was coming to one of our family members.

But more importantly, it meant that our Great Ancestral Chain was in danger and that all the gold we had within was in danger of falling into the Shadow Lands.

So our council of elders sat down and did some serious talking. Three of the tribe's most eligible daughters were being lured by Beng, and if something was not done about it, our people's future was looking grim.

The elders knew the answer had to be within the riddle.

They knew that Sonna meant 'gold' and that Rupe meant 'silver' and they concluded that one of these two sisters would be chosen to step into the Boro Dikimangro and pass her reflection along the River of Life. But so keen were they to remember that gold has a substitute that they forgot to see the true wealth of copper.

They also forgot that Horki means 'copper'.

After some considerable soul-searching, they finally realised that they were being challenged to understand the true nature of the riddle all over again.

My father had talked to Iuzio. And Iuzio had told him that if one of us was strong enough to withstand a meeting with one of Beng's Locollico spirits and Ana, then she would be the one to carry our knowledge down to the children of the future. My father had known that Beng would be attracted when we all walked into that cave with our nuggets of gold. But only Iuzio had known which one of us would be chosen.

It was the greatest test for us all, especially for the council, who soon realised that they had become far too involved with the power of sacred metal rather than its inner value.

In Sonna's dream, Chi, she walked into the cave with a nugget of gold, saw the Locollico spirit and ran out again, while Rupe in her dream walked into the cave with her nugget of gold, saw the Locollico spirit, had her golden nugget eaten by the spirit and ran out again.

I, Horki, took my nugget of gold into the cave, saw the Locollico spirit, had my nugget eaten by him and my soul blinded by Ana's light and ran out of the cave again, but eventually went back, driven by the qualities of the sacred metals which I had found within myself.

Yes, it was my anger, my courage and my sadness which put me in touch with the qualities of the sacred metals. And my water helped me to drive the dust and shadow away.

So I was finally chosen for the task because I had earned the right to carry it out.

And: *Gold is not gold when it is also copper.* Horki is chosen for the task because Horki carries the inner qualities.

Copper holds subtle secrets which we do not always see, Chi, so long as we nurture them within. And when copper is found within, then all three metals will humble themselves and shine in a way they have never shone before.

But can you see the gold in me shining? Can you see the copper? No, of course you can't see any of it, not unless you see me with your inner eyes. If you look at an individual with your inner eyes you are likely to see the existence of those qualities, or the absence of them.

It is far better to see that copper, silver and gold are an integral part of the earth and all things, and that the removal of these precious metals from the earth and all things will so easily strip away life.

Yes, Chi, that which we believe will be greater will often be lesser, and that which we believe will be lesser will often be greater.

In other words, never judge a parcel by its wrapping, or you may believe that power is contained where it is not.

Think about this. You will have a lot of words to carry about with you, won't you?

Always take your thoughts to the river. You will understand them more there, because the river will help them to flow, rather than remain stuck in your mind, moving neither one way nor the other. Thoughts are like raindrops, Chi, like waves. To understand them well, the motion of water needs to course through them.

Remember that the spirit of gold is destined to release her dark power. As Iuzio said, people will be looking for her lustre rather than her qualities. And as the Great Curse begins to move across the centuries like a black cloud, so many people are going to be eating gold. And that will cause this beautiful and wise spirit to turn her back upon everyone. And then people will know her wrath.

You are going to hear people cursing those gold tokens they carry about with them, Chi.

And the dark Lowerworld and the bright Upperworld will become paved with those tokens, more and more tokens filling every crack and crevice. And blindness will prevail, because no mortal can live in a world where so much gold is winking at them day and night without having their sight taken away. People will no longer use the tokens as a pledge, or to give their word on a bargain; they will no longer use them to let others know that they mean what they say. In the future they will use these gold tokens purely to buy for themselves whatever they desire, no matter what bad luck or bad magic it is destined to bring them, and no matter whether they have earned the spirit of gold's blessing or not. This is already happening in every market-place in every great city and town, Chi, in the places where I tell my stories. We Egyptians know it is already going on, because we keep our eyes wide open.

And because of what will be going on in the Upperworld and the Lowerworld, the Middleworld, where we all live, will be hidden. No one will see it any more, because ancient memory will have faded. And Beng's curse will be complete. And the very worst thing is that the Upperworld and Lowerworld will both be mistaken for the Middleworld and for what is normal and sensible and good.

Oh dear, Chi, what a mess it is all destined to become.

But so long as you remember that the Middleworld is where we all really need to be – that is, within that place that is in between the heavens and the bowels of the earth – you will be alright. So many will have fallen down into the dark chasms of the Lowerworld and taken up residence there, they'll swear that it is the Middleworld itself. And when you think about this, it will make sense that all these people will have sunk down and down and down and will have replaced the Middleworld with the Lowerworld, for you would not find such vast quantities of gold anywhere but in the Lowerworld or under the earth, would you?

But, then, many of these fallen people will also have floated up to the sky on clouds, because they will have mistaken the sun's rays for rows of pretty tokens – so many rays of lovely golden tokens just for the taking in the early morning woodland. Oh, Chi, how happy they will be. And they will line the walls of their houses with gold, and they will be walking on gold and sitting on gold and lying on gold, because they will always need this precious metal to be winking beside them.

Yes, the Golden City will be made manifest. And Beng, its great king, will be smiling a lot.

And the spirit of gold will no doubt be sitting back and laughing at the human race. Oh, how she will laugh. But at the same time she will have a great sadness, a regret for what might have been, just as Ana does.

Imagine, Chi, finding a golden casket and within it many tokens that you know are going to make you rich beyond your wildest dreams, a casket like the one I had in the crystal ball's story. As you run your fingers through the gold, are you suddenly swimming through a pool of ecstasy? Are you swooning with passion?

This is a seam, Chi.

And Kam, the spirit of the sun, and his daughter, the spirit of gold, are listening as I speak. Talk to these spirit ancestors and promise them that you will learn the lessons they give you about seams. Because if you are living in a world of tokens you will need to remember that the spirits of Kam and gold are contained within those tokens and these ancient influences still govern them.

Don't ignore this seam within the Great Fabric of Life, Chi. For humans will need to release the spirit of gold back into her father's hands if anything is to change for the better.

* * * * *

So, when I was just thirteen, I passed the great test that was set for me by Iuzio and the spirit of gold. And I became proud.

And now I am acting out my role, playing my part in taking our people towards their ancient homeland within the Otherworld, just as my father did, and his father before him, and all the many fathers, beginning with Iuzio, who is really the oldest father I have.

And there will be many generations, Chi, before you too step into the Long Reflection, before you also play your own role. Yet your role is coming. I will continue to believe that it is coming.

It has taken me a long time to learn the ways of the wise from my elders. We cannot escape passing from child to adult, Chi, from immaturity to maturity, and ultimately through all those pains that children must leave behind. Otherwise we are destined to remain immature forever – meaning we will become fitting bait for Beng. We must start embracing all those things we constantly push away: things like responsibility, the need for comfort, expectations, rebellion and the thief within, or trying to take that which you have not rightfully earned, including wealth, beauty and power.

Know that very few are prepared to say goodbye to immaturity. And that is why there will always be very few wise men and women in the world.

I have to tell you that after our sickness had passed, I talked openly with my sisters about my little nugget of gold and to my surprise both of them denied ever having seen me carrying a nugget of gold before. All our nuggets were dreamed, they insisted, as they had only seen their own nuggets in their dreams. I told them mine was real enough because Iuzio had given it to me. But when I reminded them that I had showed it to them many times as a child, they still assured me they had never seen me with a nugget of gold before.

So I concluded that I must first have fallen off the edge of the land and entered the Otherworld at six years old. And then I fell off the edge again when I was thirteen. And I have fallen many times since, whenever Iuzio has come to talk to me, as he does often.

Everyone has a nugget of gold deep inside themselves, he has told me. But most don't remember that it is there, and if they do they cannot be bothered to look for it. 'Your memory is strong, Horki,' he told me, 'because you know how to value and honour gold.'

I am proud that he tells me these things.

So I polish the little golden nugget daily, Chi.

Par, my husband, lies sleeping beside me now as I think of you. He is a kind and thoughtful person and I could never think of sharing my life with any other man. Our two small children play outside the tent. They are happy, and as I look over at the hazy mountains through the open flap of our tent, I wonder which one of my children will carry our knowledge on after I am gone. I wonder which one will meet Iuzio and step into the Long Reflection.

One day my time will have passed and my child's time will all too soon have passed as well. Prepare yourself, Chi, because your own time is coming. It may seem a long way from here. But I am certain, yes, I am certain now that you will appear, as the seventh of the seventh one in our line.

And that will be something to celebrate.

Sometimes I talk long into the night with Par. And we both talk about you as being part of our family. We feel for you.

Par understands the ways of the Old Land well. He

understands that the time is coming when it will be far more difficult to step into the Long Reflection and far more difficult to pass our knowledge down, because he knows, as we all know, that the Locollico spirits are gathering strength all the time, waiting for an opportunity to enchant and capture souls.

Par looks with me sometimes when we go to the river. He looks at his own face and laughs. I love him because he reminds me of Kam, the spirit of the sun.

So we both remain alert, and we teach our children to remain alert, and to use their wits. We teach them the valuable skills of Akahna and we warn them against becoming halfwits. We also teach them how to look into the water to see their own faces. Sometimes they pull tongues at themselves, as their mother used to do.

You may also want to pull tongues at your reflection, Chi. But that is how it should be. Never take life too seriously. It is far better to laugh at yourself, as all your ancestors do.

The best way to avoid the Locollico is to laugh, but also to keep looking at your reflection every day. And if you do not have any water, then you must use a looking-glass. But don't just look. You must really *look*. And if you feel you don't like yourself, ask for Iuzio to come and give you strength – ask for all those in the Long Reflection to gather together to help you along. And we will come, if we know you are calling to us. The Locollico do not like it if they know we are standing together. And Beng will leave us alone then. So remember to laugh, cry and keep your water flowing, Chi. And remember not to accept beakers from strange people. And you must not forget what Iuzio said: your inner water will always keep you safe.

I rest my hand on my belly now and I smile. For I know instinctively that the one who will carry our knowledge forward, the one who is destined to meet Iuzio and to step into the Boro Dikimangro, is still inside me, waiting to be born. I am at an early stage yet, but I know that this baby will be a girl and I know that she will make a contribution to your own life so many years from now.

So now you will, I hope, understand why it has been necessary for me to talk to you in the way I have done. You will, I hope, have a stronger idea of what your ancient grandmother is all about.

And Chi, I just want to see something of you in the river one more time before we cross the near water, so that I can remind myself that you are really there.

* * * * *

We are about to step onto the sheet of silk bearing the dancing stars. I stand on a hill and see those stars being tossed into the air upon the distant ocean, just as my father saw them all those years ago in his vision. He was standing on a hill too.

He was not destined to cross this water. For he died and said he would leave us in Iuzio's capable hands.

And Iuzio confirmed he would be waiting for us on the other side, that he would not desert us. He told me that my child would be born on the other side. And he said it would be difficult on the other side. But he also said that travelling west would be the only route back to our homeland in the Otherworld. He put his warm hand against my belly the last time I saw him and told me that the child within me would come to know him well.

So the water is near, the water is near, Chi, and many of us are excited by this. And we must visit the market-place one more time today so that I can finish my story before we leave.

We visit the river on the way. And I look over the water, looking for your face again. I wait a very long time before I see anything other than my own face. Then I see other faces forming: people in the past, people in the future. This is the nature of the Boro Dikimangro: all these faces you know and yet will never know.

I see the face of a man who comes not long after me. He is seven sons and daughters away. And he is like me.

He looks back at me from the water and gives a radiant smile because he is courageous and strong. I think he is handsome. And I know that he will make a fine leader, a king perhaps, who will protect our people and take them wherever they need to go.

But the faces that appear after his face wear expressions that are weary, muddled, unsure. And I know that these are people who are going to be affected by the Great Curse.

I see the face of someone young and I do not know if it is a boy or a girl, because it is a face that keeps changing. My father and I used to look at this face together and he assured me that if I looked long enough I would be able to see that this was the face of two people and not one: twins, perhaps.

And then there is the face of the very old man who looks at me in a kind and wise way but whose heart is heavy and sad. I have felt the burden he carries. Oh, I have felt it so much. And I have so wanted to lift it from him. He reminds me so much of Iuzio.

And then there is the hardy face of the younger man who always makes me laugh. How I want to dip my hand in the water to touch him, to let him know how heartening his face is.

After this the faces blur. But then I see a young woman who is sixth in the chain. She is bewildered, always bewildered. But I don't know why. I wish I could see why. I wish I could see what happens between the hardy young man and this woman, what happens to cause this bewilderment. But that is the way of the Long Reflection. It shows us only what we perhaps need to see, and no more. And we must simply do our part to help the future generations in any way we can.

And after the sixth face there are no more. For the seventh rarely appears, other than as a faint blur. And I dip my hand in the water often at this moment, when I haven't been able to see you properly, but there is never anything more there.

And then I talk to Iuzio, whose face looms up so clearly. 'Why, Iuzio, why?' I ask, as I have been asking for so many years. 'Why do I see no more children but this faint blur that taunts me?'

But he is unable to give me an answer. For he only knows what I know: that there may not be a seventh in the line, that our line may just come to an end.

But I am still going to keep hope in my heart and believe that you will be there, Chi.

And I am proud that I am an ancient grandmother to every single face I see. This thought warms me as I touch my belly again. Because you are all contained within my belly, each and every one of you, all of you contained within this one child I carry, like so many seeds within the grandmother seed. All of you will carry my blood, my spirit, my soul, my reflection.

And I put my ear down to the water now, as I always do, listening for the whispering of ancestors beneath the surface, so many ancestors talking at once, both in the past and the future. I do not hear exactly what they are saying, but I know that they talk of the ancestral realms where I am destined to go when I die. And they talk of the Otherworld which we are all destined to find beyond the near water on our journey west. 'Keep going, keep going,' they say. 'Never stop searching for your true home.'

I look beyond my face, beyond the woman that I have become, and I know also that I want to give my nugget of gold to you, Chi. I want to pass it down to you from inside myself, within the Long Reflection, so that you are always protected and so that you are kept safe and wise.

In the future people will want to be beautiful. I have seen this. They will do anything to call in the Locollico spirits and they will be only too happy to introduce them to the Golden City. Do not fall into the cunning traps that these mischievous spirits are going to lay at your feet in the future, Chi. I know that in the future it will be far more difficult to see where the traps are concealed. So keep your wits sharp.

I touch the water again now, disturbing my reflection as I send a prayer. And then all the visions are gone.

* * * * *

When I mention the nugget of gold to my audience in the market-place again, they are eager to hear the end of my story. I tell them a young prince fought for me in the caves in those hazy mountains. And just as he helped me defeat the evil spirit who dwells there, so he can help them.

I notice that the man who wanted to know if I still had the nugget is present in the crowd again. But there is no sign of the slobbering old man, which pleases Ag and my other brothers. We know that our ancient game took this halfwit back to the shadow world within himself and that we will never see him again.

Most of the people are still keen to have the answer to the riddle. And most are ready to fly off to the mountains to dig up their magical nugget of gold. And of course there isn't any gold – only that which lies dormant within them.

But they do not know that.

As usual, eyes glint and roll at the mention of the precious metal. And I know that the hunger the world is destined to develop for this metal begins right here, in this small market-place, as it begins in every small market-place all across the world.

'I no longer have the nugget of gold,' I assure my audience. I am lying, of course, because the nugget of gold is safely tucked inside me, just like the child I am carrying.

But are they able to answer the riddle?

'When is gold not gold?' I call again into the crowd.

I am thinking of Iuzio as I say this. And I am also thinking of you, Chi.

As usual, they can give me no ansswer.

'You will need to bring me the answer before midday tomorrow,' I tell them. And I know what will happen. I know that some will try to bribe me before that time.

I have not given them the answer to the riddle and I have no intention of giving them the answer to the riddle. Because for these people there is no answer. There are no proper answers because there are no proper questions.

I tell them I will return again tomorrow at midday and if no one has the answer, then the gold will remain undiscovered.

But of course I walk away from the market-place never to return. I have silver glinting in my palm again and I am laughing with my brothers and sisters as I go. The bribes have been many. And we have made enough money to carry to our destination across the water.

Our game of Akahna is done here now. We have exhausted the greedy halfwits, the slobbering old men, all those who crave beauty, power and wealth.

Ag walks with an arm slung across my shoulder now, mimicking the people he has just collected money from in the crowd, which he always does so politely that no one would believe they are bribing him; they might just believe that he is bribing them. He is as excited as I am that we are crossing the water to a new life. He is happy that we are taking a step closer to our homeland, even though he knows, as I know, that our journey is not going to be easy.

This strange new life is already beginning, Chi. From the moment we step onto that blue sheet of silk, things are going to change. And what I do now will affect what you do in the future.

So I will be thinking of you in all I do.

And I hope it will not be long before we see our homeland calling to us on the western horizon, the Otherworld beckoning us home. I hope we catch this glimpse before too many changes occur in the world and before the dark chasms of the Lowerworld begin opening up beneath our feet and people are pulled down and down and down. And I hope our people never forget who they are. I hope we are never destined to become stone and

84

dust and shadow.

Oh, how I hope.

And don't forget, Chi, that you will need to keep strong. You will need to keep saying to yourself: 'I am not dust. I am not shadow. A frog is a frog.'

You must think of our dear Iuzio. You must think of reflections. You must think of raindrops.

You must always remember.

The Thirteenth Hala: Europe

Ruslo Ruk's Tale

When the monks appear I fall down on my knees.

'Does God mean nothing to you, man?' an older member of their community asks.

I think a while and then hold my hands together in prayer.

'I renounce everything, sir,' I say. 'I am a wicked heathen learning to make amends. I will sometimes make mistakes because I do not know the way. Forgive me.'

A hand is placed upon my head in a gesture of forgiveness. I know I have spoken the words he wants to hear. I grab the hand and kiss it fervently.

'My son, my son,' the old man laughs, 'please, contain yourself.'

I know that he is flattered and wants more.

I am happy to give him more.

'Uncle,' I say, holding his hand to my cheek, '*good* sir, I am so grateful that I stumbled across this religious house along my road. I was destined to find you. I have come a long way to find you, from the lands where foolish and ignorant heathens abound. But I have found God here. And you are wonderful, uncle, you are wonderful.'

The old man is touched. 'Get up, get up,' he tells

me, like an old grandfather talking affectionately to his grandson.

I know I have made his day. But I wonder how I will ever manage to get up because there are so many items concealed in my robe they may all just clatter to the ground. I eventually move by slowly clutching my heart and stomach and groaning as I mimic a deep spiritual pain. If there is anything I have learned about monks, it is their love of deep spiritual pain.

I wear a thick robe over my peajamangris, my shirt and leggings. This brown tunic, sewn for me by my wife, is made of such thick material that it can conceal virtually anything within its deep pockets and when I wear it I merge with the forest so well that if I stand absolutely still, packs of hungry wolves will pass me by. I reason now that if these men are so busy listening to my soul expressing its pain, they will not question me.

And they don't.

Instead they are concerned with the pass I have given them, which entitles me to receive alms. It has been written by a wealthy respected man. He is a man whose word no one will dare question. And after looking at this pass the old monk summons younger monks to fetch bread, herrings and ale.

'Two barrels!' he calls with joy.

'*Two* barrels?' I hear one of their number cry, with immediate concern. There is a little criticism from another, but not enough to cause delay.

The old man is still smiling as he walks me away. I know I have enchanted him. I know I have played my part. I am clutching a small wooden cross to my heart. I intend the old monk to observe this, which he does.

'Collect the food and the barrels at the gate at sundown,' he tells me, walking with me to the outer edge of the monastery, his arm about my shoulder. 'We will leave them there for you.'

'Yes, uncle. Thank you, uncle,' I say, kissing his hand and making him chuckle all over again.

Once I am within the confines of the trees, I turn and wave. Here I do not need to act any more, because the monks have all gone. I breathe a sigh of relief as I give my robe a little shake and items of gold and silver come cascading out of it.

It is another successful visit to a monastery and a game of Akahna played as I might have played it the very first time.

* * * * *

A gaujo once asked me why we insist our boys play this terrible dreadful cruel game. (Those were his words.) And I told him that everyone is playing Akahna every day. It is just that the Egyptian is the only one who realises it.

I might have explained that people take what they desire from each other whether or not they are given permission and whether or not they are in need. I might have explained that by ritualising the stealing of sacred metals we become responsible for and answerable to all those important things we take for granted in life, such as power and position and love.

And you might understand that if a man is thirsty and a fountain of water flows over him, he will drink. But if that same man is thirsty and a fountain of water flows near him, he will almost certainly crave that water even more.

Our game of Akahna arranges that we sample what it means to take those things that are beyond us, Chi, those things that are not ours to have.

I didn't, of course, tell the man any of this. I left him standing staring in the market-place, and he may still be there today. Without the ability to reflect, you see, Chi, we risk turning to stone exactly where we stand. So when you find yourself looking at a big stone, remember that you might just be looking at a man or woman who perhaps thought a little too long about something, someone who chose not to reflect on the way life is.

And there are many things in this world which we think will be one thing when really they will be another. Look closely, because how do you know that you are looking at a tree? It may just be a human, in disguise. Yes, Chi, this will sound incredible, laughable even. But it is already happening in our world. Humans are destined to become hunters of the impossible, because they have not yet learned the consequences of taking that which is not theirs to have.

Do humans need the game of Akahna? Of course they do. Not only are they destined to become the fountains, but they are destined to become the stones and the trees and the dwellings and the oceans and the deserts and the mountains as well.

Can a man become a whole mountain? Yes, Chi, I assure you he can. He won't tell you he is a mountain if you ask him. But you will have your proof when you call his name and the mountain answers. If the mountain bears his name it will think like him and act like him and it will swear that it has been him all along and it will be only too happy to tell you his life story.

My grandmother became a little rosebush once. She adored the bush so much that she pulled it up and carried it around with her until my grandfather stole it away because he was tired of talking to a bush every evening around the campfire and was even more tired of going to bed with a bush every night. As you can imagine, this was most uncomfortable.

It is all true. Never believe that people are entirely themselves, Chi. They are easily drawn to become what they have a passion to be. And passions have a habit of running away with us.

So remember to see the mountains and the stones and even your own drinking cup exactly as they are. Do not be tempted to guzzle at the fountain.

You will hear that I am already talking to you as a strict father would. Know that I speak to my own five children in exactly the same way. This is because I am a true Egyptian and will tell you no lies. I only tell halfwits lies – but you'll already have learned that lying to a halfwit is different because it is usually necessary. And when we live in a world where lies become truth and truth becomes lies, who remembers the difference anyway? Except the Egyptians.

I believe that my experience with Akahna has helped me to become the honest man I am today. When the gold and silver came cascading out of my robe in the wood after my fiftieth game (yes, I have counted them all), it took me back to my first ever game, which also took place in a monastery. But had my first game been played by all the rules, I might never have found myself here in England, in the Sussex Weald, lying in this field in the warm sunshine, scratching my beard with pleasure, with a blade of grass stuck between my teeth and with my people camped safely around me. Who knows where I might have landed and what road I might have travelled?

You will hear me talking a lot about roads, Chi – life's roads, fortune's roads, love's roads, power's roads and all the imaginary roads that are in between.

There are a few things I need to say about roads and I need to do this before I tell you about that first game of Akahna.

Our people have a saying that the road that brings you always carries you away.

This basically means that all roads ahead look alike until they become the roads that are behind. For they are an enchantment until we know what they are really all about. The road *carries you away*, Chi, meaning it tempts you into believing that it is something other than it is.

Yes, the phrase contains a little trickery, in true Egyptian fashion, and as most things do in life, I'm sure you'll agree.

You will often hear me falling back on this old saying of ours when I am talking about Akahna, for all games also look alike until they become the games that are behind. How tempting they look, how much fun they appear to be, before you know what they are really all about.

And if you have trouble understanding this, just stop and reflect upon my grandmother and her rosebush. How wonderful it seemed with its beautiful perfume and its pretty flowers. Beware the beautiful perfume and the pretty flowers, Chi.

Some people put off the past, you see, and carry along the things they are meant to leave behind, so that these end up walking alongside them into the future, eating with them and even sleeping with them in their beds.

The rosebush that brings you always carries you away!

Need I say any more?

I do not quite know yet if you are female, Chi, because when I look at you in the water, you are quite difficult to see. But if you are female, know that you will be spared that difficult game called Akahna, although females have been known to play the game with skill and with great relish.

My mother enjoyed playing Akahna whenever my father displeased her. She could always catch him out, taking his favourite piece of silver from under his sleeping head. He openly said that she was better at the game than he was and for that reason I always hoped I would play the game as well as my mother, rather than as badly as my father.

As my own time of understanding these things approached, as my own Jal Raht initiation, which happens to us at puberty, came knocking at my door, I felt a new power emerging within me. Egyptians say that a boy's initiation must take place at exactly the right time: when he begins having problems with fountains.

Elders will begin watching and listening for the relevant changes as the boy's blood thickens, as his voice deepens and as his hair grows long. It is believed that if he is not *caught* at the right moment his newfound passion will spill out of him and over everyone around him. It is said that his eyes will roll with the pleasure that this new power brings and his spirit will become like the spirit of a wild horse when it is at full gallop. If care isn't taken, he will have lost himself before he has even had a chance to find himself. But there is one thing for certain, Chi: his new-found passion will be encouraged and greatly understood.

You might, however, ask: Why do Egyptians play the game of Akahna out in the world and not just among themselves?

Well, in earlier days elders acted as halfwits for a boy. But the time came when no one needed to do that any more because there were so many halfwits occupying the world. Like many, I was glad about this, because I preferred to play Akahna away from the watchful eyes of elders.

I didn't want elders to know what I was thinking, because I was obsessed with roads. I thought about roads every day and dreamed of roads every night. I had long had a fascination for our sacred road that stretched west. Some said it did not exist, but I loved this road because it seemed to travel far up into the sky; it was enduring and direct, and yet seemed to go nowhere.

There was no doubt in my mind that I was going to travel this ancient road when I grew up, and maybe even go beyond it. When tales were told which had the road as their central theme I would sit and watch this magical road snaking up out of the campfire westward into the dark night sky. At dusk it might be coloured red by the rays of the setting sun. At dawn (yes, some of our stories went on all night and sometimes into the following day), it might disappear into the morning mist. But whenever and however I saw it, there always sat upon it the most beautiful and alluring woman anyone had ever seen. She was swathed in mysterious billowing veils and was constantly calling to me to get up and follow her.

Some of my family laughed at this vision and said that the man in me was simply stirring. Others called this woman a shadow woman and the road a shadow road. If many shadows all lay down together side by side, the elders said, they could form roads that could trick and bewitch you. The elders also told me that there were roads that stretched from one end of the earth to the other and roads that stretched from one end of the sky to the other. There were roads that stretched from the earth to the sky and from the sky down to the deepest regions of the earth. But many of these were not true roads, so you had to be careful when looking for that legendary road that led west. For if you didn't look hard enough, you might just miss seeing all the shadows shuffling about and lining up, getting ready to lie down together just so that they could fool you. And if you ended up walking along one of these roads, you could find yourself walking across millions of miles of shadows that dissolved under your feet with every step you took. And this would ultimately lead you nowhere.

So the road that might bring you could also very much carry you away.

I would need to make sure that the western road *was* the western road.

But nothing anyone ever said could deter my enthusiasm to find and walk this fiery road. And the veiled woman continued to wave her alluring finger at me through every story I ever heard.

So, at fourteen years old, when setting out to play my first game of Akahna, I was warned not to follow roads or women. I was told to keep my face turned away from the west. I was advised to look out for frogs.

They told me to wash myself in the river seven times before my game began.

And then I was given a riddle, which would, they said, help me become the man I was destined to be.

This is the riddle, Chi:

I stand tall, taller than the rambling hedgerow but smaller than the sky. I snake my way along roads that go deep down into the earth but I also fly high on the roads that travel with the wind. I have the desire to spread my seed along the roads of birth and the tendency to wilt as I move along the roads of death. I have a warm brown solid

*body and a spirit that is older than anything you will find. I
am travelling all the time and yet always I stand still.*

Who am I?

Does the riddle give you a clue to my name, Chi?

Do you understand what I am trying to say to you?

* * * * *

I have always had to be careful how I move, because I move
fast, and often without invitation. What moves without
moving, Chi? This is another clue to my name; you could
say that it is a riddle within a riddle. But its answer is also
what I needed to learn when I was young.

I had it in mind to give these riddles to the group of
Benedictines who collected around me when I entered their
church. I wanted to impress them with something so clever
that they would let me go – because I knew my game of
Akahna had already gone hopelessly wrong.

I had imagined, foolishly, that the church would be a
good place in which to play the game. It was, after all, on a
road that led east. But as I stood there, naïvely blinking
at the monks gathering around me, I thought I no longer
wanted to become a man. I was quite content being a child.

The monks had already raised their brows in horror
when I told them I had entered their holy church looking
for Deevel, which I thought was the best excuse to give
them. Deevel was a most ancient and sacred spirit to us.
Because I was so young I was not to know of the unsavoury
connotations associated with the word.

An older monk drew me aside and in a polite
whisper asked me if I had ever heard of God.

And after thinking about this for some time, I
shook my head.

How could I tell him that in my own community
the word provided entertainment on quiet evenings around
the campfire?

Some of the monks began shuffling about in
agitation, as if unnerved by my presence. Others talked in

hushed whispers. Most of them pitied me. I knew without doubt that they had a passion to convert me. It wasn't often that a child of savages had stumbled upon their holy ground in this way.

One of them soon braced himself and stepped forward, clearing his throat, the noise echoing up into the giant stony void and rafters above him.

'Tell us about this, this Deevel, boy,' he announced, giving a deliberate shudder as he spoke, as if spitting out a fly which had accidentally flown into his mouth. He crossed himself afterwards, speedily and graciously, with his eyes closed. Others were quick to do the same.

I stared at him. He looked back at me from out of a pale ghoulish face brought to life by the flickering beeswax candles around him. I had spent a long time looking at the gargoyles outside before stepping into the church and now began making comparisons.

Another of the monks kept fingering the torn sleeve of his habit, trying to intensify my guilt over the handiwork I had performed upon him earlier with my knife. He had come upon me unexpectedly, put a hand on my shoulder and alarmed me. As I had lifted an arm to defend myself, I had accidentally caught his sleeve with my blade. He had then screamed so loudly that his friends had come rushing out of every corner in the belief that their brother was being attacked.

Only after they had calmed him had I mentioned Deevel, largely as a distraction. I had to stop them from questioning me about my presence in the church. There had been a problem, you see, Chi, because when I first entered the church someone else had been leaving it, another boy, his arms laden with silver, including a most decorative silver chalice. He had not looked at me as he passed, but left me to face the monks alone.

Had he also been playing the ancient game of Akahna?

I prayed that no one would blame me for the theft.

But it didn't matter, because all they wanted to

95

talk about was Deevel.

So I found myself having an audience with a group of Benedictines in a most unexpected way. Their curiosity was infectious. More and more brothers stepped up to join them, looking me up and down almost as though they wanted to poke me to ensure that I was real.

They saw before them a boy with long dark hair, wearing a bright yellow shirt, baggy blue leggings and yards of red wool, with henna painted on his face, hands and bare feet, and many luck beads wound around his neck, wrists and ankles, in strings.

I was not the kind of sight they usually beheld in their church.

'None can compare with God, boy,' one of the older men was announcing. Others were agreeing with him. Their voices echoed up into the church's great stony void and lingered there. Every time someone spoke I found myself looking up into the carved ceiling, looking for the voices, or their spirits, fascinated by the echoes that played above my head.

Had the spirits of the voices been captured by the great vaulted ceiling, enabling the men to speak to me from so high up in the air?

I pointed up at the ceiling and raised my brows in wonder. 'Avali,' I said, and they looked at each other and frowned, not understanding. They crossed themselves once again.

I looked down at the gaudy coloured patterns of stained glass dancing over the tiled floor. The spirits of these colours were attempting to speak to me in my own ancient language.

'We are spirits of the sunlight,' they said. 'We are laughing at these monks because they keep crossing themselves so much they are going to wear holes in their chests.'

'Has no one ever taught you that?' the older man was asking.

'Taught me what?' I said, bringing my attention

back to him.

I had stepped to my left in an attempt to see the colours a little more clearly, but the monks there had suddenly closed ranks, believing that I was trying to escape. And when I stepped to the right, my passage was barred in exactly the same way.

The old monk was sighing with exasperation. 'Has no one ever taught you that God is *all*?' he explained.

'All?' I asked. 'All what?'

He clicked his tongue against his palate and shook his head.

'We have never before captured one of the Devil's own,' the man who spat flies was meanwhile announcing with great amusement. He was a lanky man with stony brown eyes and a large Adam's apple. He was quickly reprimanded by one of his superiors for laughing at me. And I was glad.

'Alright, I'll tell you about Deevel if you'll tell me about God,' I finally bargained, just to bring this encounter to an end.

This was a good move, as it caused the group to produce a young monk from its centre. He stepped forward and smiled as he said, 'I think that would be a splendid idea.'

This was Brother Peter, the almoner, a respected member of the community who was accustomed to dealing with poverty-stricken faithless heathens at the gates – a category I was very quickly slotted into. He would teach me so much that I am still grateful for today.

Back then, I was relieved when this amiable brother suggested the monks escort me back to the gate. Before I left, though, I had to rush to stand in the glow of the dancing lights that coloured my shirt and leggings so that I could dance up and down like a fool. The lights sang to me and drove their colours in and out of my eyes and my soul. And Brother Peter stood patiently by, watching and smiling, doubtless pitying this being who was half-child half-man, and probably believing, I am now sure, that the 'Deevel' in this boy's soul would need to be exorcised before the heathens he was living with damaged him forever.

I liked Brother Peter. He smiled where other monks frowned. He grinned where other monks grimaced. He insisted I return for religious instruction as soon as I was able. He put a hand on my shoulder as he said this.

I heard myself agreeing, although I couldn't possibly know what I was saying while I was so young and while so many lights were enchanting me and dancing in my eyes.

When we arrived back at the gates, the lanky monk volunteered to escort me back into the forest, even though I had told him I could go by myself.

'I will lead you,' he said.

But as soon as Brother Peter and most of the other monks had disappeared, oh Chi, oh Chi, what did he do? He insisted on putting a rope around my neck.

Yes, Chi, I am serious. When no one was looking he produced a rope, put it around my neck and pulled me along like a dog, jerking me one way and then another and sometimes even knocking me down, purely so that he could drag me up off the ground again.

Two of his friends were accompanying him, shooting glances back at the monastery gate to ensure that no superiors were watching them. One of them was the monk with the ripped sleeve. And all of them made it clear that I was not welcome by hitting me with small sticks.

Their attempts to chastise me were feeble, playful rather than brutal. But still the experience was humiliating. The lanky man yanked me along, hurting my neck badly, and I only prevented myself from choking by keeping the rope slack with my fingers.

Once the rope was removed, I was left coughing and spluttering on the ground, demeaned beyond words as they began to walk away.

But then I felt my new manly power coursing through my veins and surging up within me, an anger I had never felt before, and I stood up and called out to them, halting them immediately.

Then I *looked* at them.

Yes, Chi, I mean I looked at them in the old Egyptian way.

This means I called the Evil Eye to my aid, because the Evil Eye is always wandering about somewhere, usually travelling one of those transparent roads, waiting for someone to bond with her. The Evil Eye, the dark lady whose name is Bakterimaskri Yak, minds her own business until someone begs her assistance. Now she had come to my aid.

So I announced, with a throat that was still hoarse, that each one of the monks would now begin turning to dust by steady degrees: first to wood, then to wood chippings, then to fine dust. (I didn't want them to turn to stone because I thought that would be much too good for them.)

They laughed at this, and in some ways I wanted to laugh with them, but I held on to my composure, my eyes wide and fixed on them all the while as I informed them that from now on they should look for signs of great splinters appearing in their skin.

My dark eyes seared into them (remember that very few people, Chi, like to have the darkness of an Egyptian's eyes boring into them) as I told them that by the time five years had passed their souls and bodies would have become mere powder. And I told them also that Beng and Ana and the Locollico were about to take them home. This was a spell that was irreversible, I said. There would be nothing any of them could do to break it.

Then I walked a wide circle around them, speaking in my own language and sometimes speaking in theirs, so that they understood what I was saying. I informed them that they were now enjoying one of the most powerful curses on earth. And I dragged a stick behind me, sealing their fate within the circle.

'A frog is a frog!' I shouted, my arms in the air, repeating the words three times, as all our people did, so that I would protect myself from the curse I was laying. And I saw their faces turning white as I pointed a finger at each of them, crying loudly: 'You will die! You will die! You will die!'

And it was only then that they didn't think it funny any more. It was then that one of them covered his head and dropped, quivering, to his knees, weeping and whimpering like a baby. Then another dropped to his knees so that he could pray.

This made me feel very powerful and very strong. I revelled in the power I had found.

'You will forget now,' I told them with an unforgiving sneer. 'You will forget *everything*.'

I picked up a handful of soil, letting it fall through my fingers as I crumbled it in my palm.

'Dust,' I told them, grinning at each one just as the gargoyles grinned from the corners of their church. 'This is what you will become now. When five years have passed, you will all become dust, and then mere shadow.'

The lanky man had not moved a muscle. Yet he was staring at me with a fear I had never seen on a man's face before. This made me realise the strength of my power. I told him that he would feel the earth moving beneath his feet and the sky caving in above him. I would cause the birds to fly out of the trees and drop down from the sky for no reason. I would cause animals to run backwards.

And even though a bird was flapping up out of a tree just as it normally would, and even though a fly was buzzing around his head just as it normally would, I saw in his eyes his belief that all the wood was under my power. He flinched as the twigs and leaves moved. He cowered as the breeze ruffled his hair.

When I felt my power to be absolute, I stepped away, satisfied.

Was I guzzling at the fountain, Chi? Had I been lured to travel the shadowy roads of power and arrogance? Were spirits lining up before me, getting ready to lie down to form that transparent road? I was not facing west. The veiled woman had not made an appearance. I had seen no frogs.

100

This is something for you to ponder on.

So, when the monks had gone, I turned to move away. But to my surprise I found myself walking straight into a man who had been standing directly behind me.

At first I believed him to be another monk. The colourful woollen material my face sank into gave off a wonderful aroma of sweet herbs and fresh laundering. But when I looked up at him in surprise I saw a man who was nothing like a monk at all. He was tall and had the fairest hair, the boniest cheeks, the largest jaw and the most intense blue-grey eyes I had ever seen. Both his tunic and his manner suggested that he was a wealthy man, perhaps a man of position and power.

I tried to run but he held onto my arm. 'Not so fast, young savage,' he said.

I struggled and tried to bite him, as my sister did whenever I held her against her will.

'Look, look, look,' he said, quickly, producing a ring made of horn and copper and waving it under my nose. 'Is this the kind of spoil you're looking for? Is this the kind of thing that attracts you to steal?'

I tried to bite him again, because I was not a thief – at least not the kind of thief he thought I was. But he lifted me into the air with ease, carried me to a ditch and threw me down.

Now there was no way I could escape because I was lying face down with one of his feet pressing into my back.

And there I remained for a long time.

* * * * *

'Are you ready to listen now?' he asked.

I had no choice. My face had been squashed against the earth for a number of minutes.

I had worked out by this time that he was a man of position, a nobleman, perhaps even a knight, because he smelled like a knight. Wealthy people and lords and knights smelled of a mixture of sweet herbs and sweat, of grace and brutality, of nobility and coarseness which brought a tingle to the nostrils that could make you want to sneeze.

He was speaking to me in French, and although I didn't speak the language well, I knew enough to converse. Here in southern Europe we were a long way from France, but the French tongue reached our camps whenever people visited shrines across the water and asked for portraits of their holy saints to take with them. Our people were adept at carving and in exchange for coins and gifts could carve any face on a wooden tablet.

'My father will come looking for me!' I tried to shout. 'My people will be here soon!'

'Will they now?' the man came back at me, unimpressed, increasing the pressure of his foot. 'Those monks are my friends, you know, savage.'

Then he released me and sat back against the slope of the ditch, watching me sit up.

I saw that his long legs were covered by dark green hose and that his green woollen tunic, bearing a printed gold design, reached well below his knees. Arrogance had taken up residence in his sweeping blue-grey eyes. I had not met much arrogance before. It was a power so pure and dark that I was wholly fascinated by it.

'Is this Beng?' I thought, not without a little excitement as I examined his long green legs. I had listened to so many campfire stories about Beng, the Boro Mulo, the Great Frog, and had always longed to meet this fascinating and malevolent spirit.

'Do something for me,' the man said, 'and I will not only keep quiet about the theft that took place earlier in the church, but I'll grant you one thing you really desire.'

It was said that Beng offered you what you desired before he ate you. And I always thought that sounded exciting. Was I about to be gobbled up alive? Would my people never see me again? But I wasn't a thief.

'I didn't steal anything, uncle,' I told him urgently. 'I've done nothing wrong.'

I addressed him as 'uncle' out of politeness. It was

102

how I'd been taught to address every man older than myself. I was also trying to appease him so that he might be tempted to let me go and not eat me after all.

'You've done nothing wrong?' he echoed.

I didn't answer. His pure dark power was enchanting me again. Whenever he grinned, his jaw seemed to stretch wider than the forest itself. And I was intrigued by the strange darkness in his blue-grey eyes. Gaujo eyes were like that, one colour and another, often at the same time.

Though I didn't actually want to be eaten, I really hoped that he was a bad spirit, because I had a passion to meet one. Some of my people were said to have met the Locollico and there was one story of an ancient grandmother of mine who was very nearly gobbled whole in a cave by one of Beng's faithful sons. If I managed to make it back to camp without being eaten, a story about Beng would last for many generations and would give me enormous popularity.

'I know you didn't steal anything,' the man finally confessed. He jolted his head in the direction of the monastery. 'But they don't know that,' he added, with a sadistic glint in his eye. 'Do they? They'll believe you stole the silver if I tell them you did.'

I was sure he could hear my heart beating fast. How did he know what had taken place in the church? Had he been following me? Beng would know many things, because he was such a great spirit. He could turn himself into anything, so he might have been a pew, or a tapestry on the wall, or one of the beeswax candles right beside me in the church all the time I was with the monks. He could have entered the bodies of some of the monks themselves, as they were known to be shadowy creatures.

Now the nobleman was suggesting I follow him home. Where was 'home'? Down in the Lowerworld? Down in the darkest bowels of the earth? Some of the darker spirits, it was said, were able to take you anywhere they pleased, and it was frequently into these dark dreadful places.

I stood still and closed my eyes tightly, saying excitedly in my own language, 'A frog is not a frog. A frog is not a frog. A frog is not a frog.'

I was attempting to summon Beng or turn this man back into his original amphibious form.

'Stop your savage babbling!' he said, shaking me hard and cuffing me round the ear. 'You'll speak no heathen words in my presence unless I ask you to. Just keep quiet and follow me. You'll like what I'm going to propose.'

So I followed him 'home', which turned out to be not the Lowerworld, but the guest-house back in the monastery. I looked out for three concerned brothers, but fortunately they were nowhere to be seen. And I realised I could have run away and could have done so many things.

And isn't it strange, Chi, the way fate lures us to our destiny? If I hadn't believed that the man was Beng I might never have followed him. And if I hadn't followed him I would never have stepped out upon the road that led to the western horizon. I would never have been lying here in England in the sunshine, scratching my beard, with my people camped safely alongside me.

I would never have understood the riddle associated with my name.

* * * * *

There are twists and turns along every road, Chi. Never ignore them. These unexpected and annoying little curves are often instrumental in changing our lives for the better – although sometimes for the worse.

When I returned to the monastery I believed I would be punished for carrying out the curse on the monks. Instead I found myself seated at a long trestle table in the luxurious quarters of the guest-house.

The man, who said he wanted to be known as 'Hawk', sat opposite me as the table was laid out with a great feast. This guest-house was 'home', he said, whenever he happened to be visiting this part of the world on pilgrimage.

He didn't look like a hawk. I thought he looked more like a swan, with his snowy-white hair and his long graceful neck. He was tall and elegant like a swan, with long blond lashes that kept sweeping against his cheeks, and he had a jaw that was as strong and as powerful as a great beak. I thought him celestial and masculine at the same time. And I greatly admired the combination of these qualities.

A real hawk was sitting on a perch in the corner, looking as though he had been painted onto the far wall. And there was a strong smell of herbs under my nose each time two servants in plain newly laundered tunics tiptoed in and out of the door. Quietly and efficiently they brought in plates, bowls and knives, bowing to both of us and addressing Hawk as 'my Lord'.

I continued to address him as 'uncle', even though I still believed he was probably Beng in disguise. He didn't object. He said it made him feel we had known each other a long time and were already friends. He said he wanted us to understand one another. But as bread, cheese, a large platter of succulent cold meats and a pie containing beef, spices and a creamy almond sauce were carried into the room and laid down upon the clean white tablecloth and a plentiful supply of barley beer was deposited on the side dresser, it was difficult for me to concentrate on what he was saying.

You must understand, Chi, that I had never seen such a display of food before. I had never even sat on a chair in a room before. So this was a strange, new and unnerving experience for me, a young Egyptian savage, inexperienced in the workings of civilised life.

'Eat,' Hawk said, waving a hand to give me permission.

I wrapped my tongue and teeth around everything, savouring every single mouthful. Uncle Hawk laughed at me. I ate like a true savage, he said.

In contrast he pulled his food apart slowly with graceful, delicate fingers, fingers that belonged more on the hand of a minstrel than on a warrior, which is what he professed to be. Graceful in body and brutish in spirit – how I admired such traits.

Now and then he pointed out to me that I wasn't obliged to eat absolutely everything that was on the table. But saying this to an Egyptian is like telling him he can never again walk in the sunshine and the wind. We had to eat when we could, because we were not always fortunate in our hunting forays. So I couldn't help going back to the large platter and the pie dish for more, not because I was hungry, but because it was there and I might never have another chance to eat in this way again.

When he wasn't laughing at me, Uncle Hawk relaxed. He pulled a foot up onto his carved oak chair, casually peeling an apple and using his slender knee as a table.

Without taking his eyes off the apple for a second, he said, 'You don't believe any of this, do you, savage?'

I naturally thought he was talking about the feast and the room and the table and the chair, and nervously wiping my mouth with my sleeve, I assured him that nothing like this had ever happened to me before and was hardly likely to happen again.

But he waved my enthusiasm away.

'No, no,' he said. 'I'm not talking about the food. I'm talking about this monastery, and the way your people think. They're not fooled by any of this, are they – the religious houses, the Christian faith, the way we all live?'

I stared at him. I didn't know what to say. I had never heard a gaujo speak like this before about the gaujo world. But then I started laughing, because a rumbling was coming up from my stomach, causing me to belch. The barley beer was going to my head. I apologised.

Hawk was unforgiving. He looked at me with eyes that said, 'Stop behaving like a child and start behaving like a man, for you are in the civilised adult world now.'

Then he went on to talk about pilgrims who travelled a long way for little purpose. He told me he couldn't see how relics and collections of old bones could really do anything in so-called 'holy' shrines except enchant people into believing something was special when it was not. Then he added that he travelled for very different reasons, for his own ends, just like Egyptians.

I kept quiet. I didn't tell him that we didn't travel for our own ends, but because we wanted to return to the Old Land in the west.

'Your people poach what they can from the monks, don't they?' Hawk seemed determined to tell me all about my own people.

I became mesmerised by the peel of the apple curling sensuously down to meet the white cloth.

'Your people laugh in the face of God,' he went on. 'I admire them because they are unafraid of the darkness.'

I wanted to laugh again, for here were more facts about my people that were not at all true. My people did not laugh in the face of God, because we didn't believe a Christian god existed. And all Egyptians were intensely afraid of the darkness. But I was not going to tell him any of this.

Still peeling his apple, Hawk told me that he was an Englishman and that his brother was coming into a greater inheritance than he himself had received. His brother was a devout Christian. But he did not deserve what was coming his way because he had killed their mother.

I blinked, confused. I considered this a strange thing to tell someone you hardly knew. I didn't know what any of this had to do with me.

Then, slowly slicing some of the apple and slipping it into his great beak, Hawk said, 'What would you like, savage? What would be your greatest desire if you could choose whatever you wanted?'

I thought about this, looking up into the rafters as I did so. Up there I could see another bird, large and black, the shadow of the one that was in the corner. Again and again I looked up, wondering if this menacing shadow was an omen.

107

Yet I didn't think it would do any harm to think about what I desired. I knew it would be wonderful to return home with enough silver to prove myself a man after my first game of Akahna. But my desire to travel the western road and to take my people with me had to be the greatest desire of all. I only had to think about this to feel my blood pumping with excitement. I imagined being a warrior-king and the hero of many campfire stories in the future.

But alongside this I remembered the stories of Beng, who always wanted to know your innermost desires and dreams before he ate you. I wondered if Hawk was about to eat me; perhaps that was why he hadn't eaten much during the meal. Having just eaten such a delicious selection of food myself, I thought I was probably going to taste quite good when he finally sank his teeth into me.

'Oh, come, come,' he said, impatient at my prolonged silence. 'I know more about your people than you think. I know of the knowledge you carry. I saw the way you cursed those three brothers out there in the wood. I saw the fear in their eyes. Fear interests me, savage, especially fear of the old world. Your people have their eyes open, don't they? They see life as it is.'

I didn't reply. I was busy seeing myself standing up and running outside, and seeing him giving chase. I watched myself drawing a sword and challenging him. I was elegant and brutish. I had seen battles and had fought for women and I owned vast amounts of land. I didn't need to care. I could snap my fingers and have anything I desired and I could sit at table and peel apples over my knees. I heard myself telling my children and my grandchildren all of this. And I heard the story moving along the generations into the future and reaching the ears of many of my people in centuries to come.

Hawk threw the ring of horn and copper across the table at me. 'This is my favourite,' he said. From a pouch he took two more rings, both of them silver, and hurled these at me as well.

I looked at all three glinting in front of me. I

thought they were beautiful. Whose were they? His own? The monks'?

'They're yours,' he said suddenly. 'Take them back to your people and tell them that these treasures are the result of your game of Akahna.'

'Akahna?' I cried, looking up at him in shock. 'How do you know that word?'

He was grinning at me. The beak had stretched wide again.

'I know about Akahna,' he said. 'I know more about your people than you think. Just agree to carry out a task for me and I'll vow to do something in return. It's as simple as that. You'll have a chance to satisfy your greatest desire – like going west?'

I stood up and ran to the door. This wasn't funny any more. I really was in the company of Beng. I wondered if I could sick up the food – it could have been laced with poison – or whether it was already too late. In panic I rattled the latch of the door, trying to get out.

'How far do you think you would get?' he was saying, unruffled, still in his chair, still using his knee as a table, still sculpting his apple. He had not even glanced at me. 'Sit down, savage!'

'Let me out!'

'Sit down!'

'No, I want to get out.'

He raised his voice: *'Sit down!'*

I turned slowly, panting nervously as I stood with my back against the door.

'How do you know about Akahna?' I asked. 'How do you know about our journey west? I want to know. You *must* be Beng.'

'Who?'

Here at last was a word he didn't recognise. I saw him frown. But Beng was clever. He would not wish to reveal his own identity, would he?

When I heard the door being unlatched behind me, I was fully expecting the beautiful Ana, Beng's devoted woodland queen, to walk into the room to join him. But it was a servant, probably summoned by the disturbance.

'Out!' Hawk did not even bother to turn to look at him.

The servant disappeared again without fuss. I had heard that servants could be flogged for the slightest offence in the gaujo world. I had also heard that Egyptians could be flogged for no offence at all. What was I doing here? My excitement had caused me to become reckless. I had to get out.

'You can agree to carry out this task for me, savage,' Hawk was saying, 'or take what is coming to you when I tell the monks all about what happened to the three helpless brothers in the wood and about the silver you stole from the church.'

He was leaning arrogantly back in his chair. I stepped towards him.

'I want to know how you know all these things about my people before I agree to do anything,' I told him. 'And I want to know now.'

Slowly his face broke into a smile. 'Now?' he said, amused. 'This minute?'

At last he turned to look at me.

'Yes,' I said.

As he turned away again, still with a smile on his face, I looked at him more closely, realising how unreachable he was. If I stretched out a hand to touch him I wondered if I might discover that there was no one there. I was prepared for this. I was prepared for the worst kind of shadow. I was prepared for a complete transformation into a frog.

But all that happened was that he carried on speaking.

'I will only tell you how and why I know what I know about your people, savage, if you agree to work for me,' he said.

'Alright,' I said. I simply had to know, though I wondered whether I'd regret it.

Still lying back in his chair, he sighed, determined to prolong the suspense. Finally he said, 'First, savage, you must understand that I want you to go to England because I want you to use your Egyptian powers to curse my brother. I want things to be difficult for him. I want him to die, slowly if possible. Do you understand?'

He spoke with a very straight face and with great politeness, as if asking me to go and fetch some more barley beer from the dresser. Did he know what he was asking? An Egyptian curse wasn't something that was practised as a daily routine. And what he definitely didn't know was that I didn't know how to carry out a curse at all, even though I had just cursed the three monks in the wood. Most of what I'd said and done had been patched together from what I'd seen and heard my elders doing on dark nights when I should have been asleep. I was hardly acquainted with the Evil Eye at all. And contrary to what many believed, my elders cursed people only rarely, because it was an art which took many years to learn, an art which I, at my tender age, should not even have been meddling with. If you had not had an apprenticeship with a holy man or woman, a curse could go horribly wrong.

'Why do you ask me to curse someone for you?' I said. 'Why me?'

'Because I know of the power of the old world and I know of the power your people possess and your connection with strong magic. I saw your strength out there in the wood. I saw how you believed. You wonder how I know of your ways and your words. Well, I've met many of your people over the years, and all of them believe. The one who tiptoed past you with his spoils in the church isn't a stranger to me.'

'The thief in the church?' I cried. 'He was an Egyptian?'

He nodded.

'But I didn't recognise him. He isn't from our tribe. He doesn't even look like an Egyptian.'

'That's because he's a half-breed, but still playing

111

the game of Akahna, even if it's in places where he should never be playing it.'

'So that is how you know about our game, uncle?'

'Yes, that is how I know about your game. Div's mother is a full-blooded Egyptian. She is a mistress of mine. I see her often.'

He was sitting forward again with his hands clasped in front of his face. I knew he wanted an answer from me. I could see the iron-hard look of determination again darkening his blue-grey eyes. People rarely defied this man. He was not the type to give in without a fight.

'I know of the Egyptians' desire to go west,' he continued. 'If you know Egyptian savages well and their links with the earth, it's common knowledge. If you desire this passage west enough, my friend, I will give you a pass that will take you all the way to England. You can take some of your people with you. You'll be happy there. You'll be able to travel completely unharmed along your road, as long as you go as Christian pilgrims, doing penance like the heathens that you are. So it will be necessary to pretend that you're not quite the savages you appear to be, but decent, honest, God-fearing beggars. And then once you arrive in England you can go directly to my estate. But when you are there I want you to say nothing of this meeting, or of me. I want you to say that you were given the pass from a good man whose name you don't recall. He was a Christian man who offered you hospitality and shelter and who understood your needs to reform. It'll just so happen that you have wandered onto my estate. Then, when I return to England from my own pilgrimage, you'll be pleased to see me again, because it'll be a coincidence that you've rediscovered me. You'll fall at my feet for having been so good to you in the past. And freedom will be yours so long as you have carried out the curse and my brother is dying or dead.'

My mind was spinning. I didn't know what to say.

After a while Hawk got up to help himself to more barley beer from the side dresser and poured more for me.

112

'How do you know I would carry out this task, uncle?' I wanted to know. 'How do you know I wouldn't use the pass to reach another place?'

'Of course you'll carry out the task,' he said, with his back to me. 'Of course you'll reach England. It's in the west.'

And then, turning, he added, 'Shuri will be going with you.'

'Shuri? Is that your mistress?'

'Yes,' he said, coming back to sit at the table again. 'And Div too.'

'The thief in the church?'

He nodded.

'If Shuri and Div aren't on my estate when I return, I'll find you,' he went on. 'Believe me, I'll find you. The pass I'll give you will take you along a designated route. And Div is the most gifted tracker I've ever known. You'll never go anywhere without him knowing about it.'

He stared hard at me. He meant what he was saying.

'What do you say then?' he asked.

'Why can't Div or Shuri carry out your curse?'

'They haven't your strength of power or character. They don't believe as much as you do.'

'Can't you get another Egyptian to do it?'

'No one else has your way. No one else believes.'

No one else would be naïve enough to do such a thing I might have thrown back at him, had I been older.

But when I thought about it I realised that not a day passed in our camp without someone mentioning our journey west and our return to the Old Land. Not a day passed without someone looking along the road and yearning for the western horizon, that magical road that curled up into the sky. I was not the only one to dream of it. But perhaps I was the only one to dream of it every hour of every day.

I passionately wanted to agree to the task, regardless of the curse or any consequences that might happen as a result. The fact that he had asked me to kill a

113

man seemed inconsequential. Oh, how impulsive youth is, Chi.

He sat there, his eyes fixed on my face, willing me to say the one word he was longing to hear.

And when I finally did say it, delight flooded into his hardened face, causing him to look like an elegant swan once again.

He stood up, taking a knife out of his belt. 'Will you swear an oath with your blood that you will do this thing for me?' he asked. 'I know a savage isn't likely to swear by the grace of God.'

I stood up. 'Yes, uncle,' I said bravely. 'I will swear an oath with my own blood.'

I already felt like a warrior and a real man.

I watched him cut his finger quickly, adeptly, with his knife, dripping blood down onto the clean white tablecloth. He then passed the knife to me and I did the same, a little more clumsily, my own blood dripping down and staining the cloth in the same way. I felt no pain. I was proud to see the little pool of blood gathering in front of me. It seemed a sign that I was a real man at last.

Then Hawk lifted his goblet, and I did too, copying his every move.

'Shastiben!' he cried.

'Shastiben!' I echoed. It was a word he must have learned from his mistress, a toast to what was to come.

The bird moved in the corner. It made a strange noise and I saw a dropping fall. I drank down some of the beer. A servant stood at the door watching us, watching the blood soaking into his once-clean tablecloth.

And all I could think was, 'I'm going west. I'm going home.'

* * * * *

The wood in the new land drips now after the earlier shower of rain, reminding me of that blood dripping down so long ago. I left the sunny field because it started to rain and now

I am sitting on a hill beneath a great oak, where it is dry, looking over the sun-dazzled stretch of water on the horizon in front of me.

There are so many stories about water, Chi, about rivers and oceans and lakes and even the small droplets of rain that are strung along the underside of branches after a shower. Stories abound of the little people's gems being hung out to multiply. And this enables our rivers to swell and our Boro Dikimangro to grow big. The little people believe that if humans have no rivers they will not be able to see themselves, and if they cannot see themselves the world will fall down.

Do you believe this, Chi? I hope you do. I hope you will not forget the things your ancestors tell you, because if you forget, nothing will go well for you. And you need to remember so that our line continues. I know what is happening. I am not stupid – even though I might have seemed stupid when I was younger. I have seen the look on your face when you've appeared to me in the water. And you do not appear to me often. And I do not quite know why that is. I imagine I see within you a lack of courage, because many I have seen in the future don't seem to know what courage is. I hope you won't have forgotten fear, because then you won't have forgotten courage. Oh, how I feel like lifting your chin whenever I see your head sinking against your chest. I want to lift your face and give you hope, as any caring father would. If there is anything I could pass down to you, Chi, it would be courage.

I can tell you that when I was young my grandmother told me wonderful stories of courage whenever she talked to me about the little people, or woodland folk. Sometimes I am still running from tree to tree, counting all those sparkling watery gems, seeing how many I can count before they drip down and are taken back into the little people's homes in the realms beneath the earth. For there, deep under the earth, if you linger too long you will need to have the greatest courage of all. For that is the place where fear is worst, Chi. Once I managed to count a whole two hundred and forty-four droplets upon just a few branches, all in one morning, before the woodland folk had time to pull me down.

My grandmother told me I would come to know courage very well, along with many of the ways of the Lowerworld, and she also told me that the spirit of courage was destined to walk at my side wherever I went.

She also used to tell me that fountains and rushing water could take your reflection away if you did not learn your lessons well. You couldn't see your reflection in water that was moving, she said, only in water that was still. And I always thought that made a lot of sense. What moves but does not move, Chi? Remember what I asked you before? Remember how important our riddles are.

As I think of these words I look up into the glistening branches of the oak above me. And I ask it this same riddle. And the tree smiles at me, knowing full well what the answer is. Remember that trees know more secrets than we could ever imagine, Chi, and these secrets are passed down through their generations, and usually more successfully than we can pass anything down our own generations, because trees are not as stupid as humans. Nothing would induce them to forget.

I took a long time to learn that trees were wise and to gain just the smallest amount of wisdom from this great tree is an honour to me now.

* * * * *

After that encounter with Hawk, I moved just like a rushing fountain back through all the trees in the wood, fear rushing at my side. And perhaps for the first time I could feel the real power that was in trees. I dashed this way and that, so that none of them would catch the secrets I had and pass them on to my elders, because if trees could pass secrets on to each other, they could certainly pass them on to the wisest of human beings.

I was clutching the three bright rings which I was

116

to present to my elders in pretence that I had played our sacred game of Akahna in the church.

But when I arrived back at the camp and stood in front of my grandmother, she said just one word: 'Fountains!'

I gasped, and everyone gasped, for we all knew exactly what she was talking about.

I hung my head in shame. I could hide nothing from my grandmother. She always sat in our great council bender, dripping with gold and beads and feathers and shells and the hair of horses and looking supremely ugly, which in a strange way always made her look tremendously beautiful. She had been admired by many men in her youth, but now that her face had become lined and some of her teeth had fallen out, she, like many old holy women, carried her age with great dignity and pride, and that gave her an ugliness that was simply an unrivalled beauty.

Now, as I stood in front of her, she spat seven times on the ground. My grandmother always enjoyed spitting, but never spat without good reason. So I knew she was intensely displeased with me.

Then she turned her attention to the ring made of horn and copper and afterwards to the two silver rings, looking at all of them for some time while everyone waited, holding their breath. Then she spat another seven times.

And then she smiled, her great ugliness shining through. The spitting, she said, was for my dance with the fountains. She wanted to protect herself. And the smile, she said, was for the rings, because she thought they were beautiful.

I smiled too, hoping she would be fooled.

But then she held up the ring made of horn and copper, the one Uncle Hawk had said was his favourite, and I knew she would hear the voice of the ring speaking to her. After the special relationship she had built with the rosebush in her earlier years, she had learned to speak the language of many things, and sacred metals had become her speciality.

117

My mother started trying to kiss and hug me, praising me for what I had done, whatever it was, perhaps in an attempt to distract everyone from the path my grandmother was taking. But as I looked over her shoulder at my grandmother silently looking at the ring, I feared the worst.

'This ring speaks of a place far away,' she soon announced in a loud and dramatic voice, the kind of voice that also said: 'This is serious and will change our lives and none of you will ever be the same again.'

I sighed, closed my eyes and awaited my fate.

'This ring tells me its real master is one who cheats and lies his way through life. Fountains, boy, fountains! That is what the ring is saying to me. It knows all about fountains.'

Everyone was staring at her by this time, somewhat nervously. Some were biting their nails.

She went on: '"I do not belong here," the ring is saying. "I have been stolen from someone in another land." It also says that it did not come to this camp through the sacred game of Akahna.'

Gasps abounded once again. And I saw no reason to lie any more. Dropping to my knees, I confessed everything, from the monks leading me like a dog through the wood to Uncle Hawk's feast and his asking me to lay a curse in England in order to kill a man. I confessed that I had not played the game of Akahna at all. I had failed in every way.

The council, some fifteen people, including my mother and father, sat looking at me in silence for a very long time.

'The council will be the judge,' they said finally. 'Step outside, so that we can decide what should be done with you.'

'This is a difficult situation,' I heard them say as I walked out through the door. 'Nobody has ever played their first game of Akahna in this way before.'

When I was called back inside I was told that I had

118

invited a strange spirit to enter my soul. I had invited the fountain to gush over me and the only way I could understand what was going on was to take myself out to the forest so that I could think this over on my own. I was to spend three days and three nights there, returning only after the fattening moon had become full.

My meeting with Hawk might yet turn out to be an auspicious omen about travelling west. But before I became too excited by that idea, I should think about it. No one could be certain about anything until some answers had been found through clear visions.

I was reprimanded for agreeing to take a journey west, for agreeing to take *any* journey without first consulting my elders, and for attempting to cheat at our sacred game. I was also going to have to think over what I had agreed to do when I reached England. But if I could allow my own spirit and my dreams to speak to me in the quiet of the forest, I might understand the deeper implications of what was happening to me and what I had agreed to do. And I could at last receive some guidance.

'Go,' they said.

So I went.

I took myself to other side of the forest, where the trees met the river. And there I set up camp, building myself a bender and lying under the fattening moon.

'What have I done?' I kept thinking, as I lay looking up at the stars. 'What have I done?'

* * * * *

I stayed alone on the edge of that forest for three days and three nights, praying as hard as I could to every spirit I knew. I went over everything that had happened to me. Travelling west had for so long been my greatest dream, but I now felt that Uncle Hawk had cheapened all those beautiful images of the road into the western sky and the veiled woman. He had made a fool out of me. The monks had made a fool out of me. There had been a conspiracy

119

between all of them and everyone had taken advantage of my age and my being an Egyptian 'savage'. All I longed to do was erase the whole experience from my memory.

I was young then, Chi, too young. Hawk, who must have been at least thirty years of age, should have been old enough to know better than to burden a boy with his own problems, for these were problems that even a man of my own age now – forty-two – would find difficult. He should, unquestionably, have been sorting his life out for himself. And if I knew anything at that time, it was that I was not the only one who was having a dance with fountains. Uncle Hawk needed the firm hand of my grandmother as much as I did.

But fate can deal us lucky cards, Chi, when we least expect them. Egyptians are great believers in luck and great believers in fate. Lady Fate was watching over me, although I would not earn the luck without the usual amount of hardship and the many dances with shadows it brings.

But not knowing what was to come, all I could do was pray that my spirit and my dreams would speak to me.

So, at night in my solitary camp I lay beside my fire staring up at the bright moon, burning herbs, inhaling their perfume and asking for visions to come. In the mornings I looked over the great valley and the river beyond, listening to the haunting cries of eagles and hawks and wondering which road would eventually pick me up and carry me away. Would it ultimately be the road that led west? I doubted it more and more as time went by.

Pictures of England curled up in the smoke of my fire and I mourned them as they almost spluttered into life and then faded away again. They glimmered for just a second, but long enough to torment me. I saw a castle etched on a skyline with tall towers and flying banners and magnificently painted walls. Yes, England became a single castle. And sometimes the land surrounding this castle became the most fierce magical land, with great dragons stalking the villages, eating up maidens in their path, and powerful ugly little people weaving their terrible magical spells in broad daylight. How I cherished ugliness. Other times the land around this castle was a more righteous land, with people being rewarded for acts of subservience, and brutish knights strutting about with elegant ladies on their arms, and gargoyle monks out on the streets flogging poverty-stricken heathens.

But all of this came to me in great flashes and did not linger.

I longed for England to be that place where gems were strung along every branch of every tree. I wanted it to be that place where no one had bad dreams any more, where our line continued on. I had heard so many stories about the end of our ancient bloodline and the end of the sun in the sky. Some of them had been passed down from the ancient grandmother I have already spoken to you about, a woman who thought it especially important that we preserved our Great Ancestral Chain. And although I didn't understand the full implications of those ancestral links, I knew enough to want to help this great chain survive.

I cried a good deal over those three days, with only the moon and the stars to comfort me. I cried for myself and for our people. I cried enough to make a whole new river, Chi.

And on the third night I admitted defeat and prepared my things for the return to camp on the following morning. Having received no great visions or powerful dreams, I knew I would have to face the prospect of never being trusted again or even being thrown out of the tribe. Few Egyptians tolerated deceit within their tribes.

But late that night a dream at last came to me.

In the dream it was quite dark and the moon was rising full and golden on the eastern horizon. A man came to stand beside me, filling the space of the moon.

I offered him a drink of water and he hesitated but finally took the clay beaker from me, sipped the water slowly, then sat down and warmed himself with a hand held out to the fire. And when I asked him who he was, he said, 'I come from the place you have not yet found, Ruk, but it

121

is also the place you never really left behind.'

Surprised that he knew my name, I stood up quickly and looked all around, believing him to be one of Hawk's men come to spy on me.

He was holding out the cup to me, having finished the water. 'Thank you,' he said, smiling.

I took the beaker from him. 'Do I know you, uncle?' I asked quickly. I was thinking of all the people who might have come to spy on me.

Squatting at my fire in the Egyptian way, he looked into the flames with his deep blue eyes. The colour of his eyes confused me, as I had never seen an Egyptian with eyes the colour of the summer sky and hair the red of flames.

I sat down again carefully, not taking my eyes off him for one moment.

Then stranger things happened, Chi, as they can in dreams.

A sudden gust of wind blew over us both from the west. It disturbed my fire, which flickered violently for just a few seconds. It disturbed my hair, which blew across my eyes so that I couldn't see. But most of all, it disturbed my soul.

A leaf fluttered past me after the wind had calmed, the sun went behind a cloud when there was only darkness, a small wave leapt out of the river when the water was very still. Everything became topsy-turvy. And I began to see many things which seemed not to belong to the time and place I was in. I didn't know if this was day, night, winter, summer or spring.

'A frog is a frog!' I cried out loud, holding on tightly to my dagger, my hand already becoming clammy. For I had the terrible thought that this was not a dream, but a nightmare. I might be in the presence of a powerful spirit, perhaps a Locollico spirit. When a wind blew very suddenly across you and then calmed again like this, and when things defied the laws of nature like this, it meant that spirits were in your presence. I kept Beng in my mind. And by now I had lost my passion to meet this malevolent spirit. In fact I was beginning to feel that I was reaping the harsh rewards of my desire to dance with him.

'You are a spirit,' I bravely told the man in front of me.

'Yes, Ruk,' he admitted, turning his great dancing blue eyes upon me.

'And you have found me in my dream, uncle?'

'No, Ruk. This is not a dream.'

I stood up again quickly, picked up a handful of soil and threw it over my head, once, twice, three times for protection, also throwing some into my mouth. I spat on the ground seven times. I did everything I had ever seen anyone in my tribe do when trying to protect themselves. Then I pinched myself until it hurt, until I made myself yelp, because if this wasn't a dream, then this spirit had to be more powerful than I could possibly imagine.

'Calm yourself, Ruk,' he said. 'Let us talk.'

I eased myself down slowly, ready to leap up if I needed to, one hand on my dagger, the other on the soil.

And then I listened as the spirit told me that his name was Iuzio. He told me that he was not a Locollico spirit, but an ancestor of mine. I was about to set out on a very long road with our people, he said. And I would need to travel across the land with my spirit rather than with my legs. I would need to understand the nature of fountains as I'd never understood them before, because I would travel out from the place where my reflection lived within me, not from the place where I lived within my reflection. I needed to go beyond what I saw whenever I looked at myself in the water.

I didn't understand most of this, especially the part about reflections. So Iuzio invited me to go to the river with him.

As we walked, I kept one eye on him and another on the moon. The moon could lead you astray when she was full, I had heard. Her roads were the most dangerous roads of all. If you travelled along them you could become one of her knights, for she collected great bands of warriors around her who were all ready to defend her and champion her needs. And her needs were many.

Men fell hopelessly, stupidly, in love with the moon. And some of the greatest sorcerers had been led down the wildest paths of chaos after being unknowingly enchanted by this irresistible beauty of the night sky. And yet it was also said that if you became a knight of the moon, a knight of Shon, it was the highest honour. In earlier times, they told me, when women spoke with the tongue of the moon and men spoke with tongues of fear, men worked hard to earn such a favour. They had to undergo a great many tests and initiations, and if they failed they risked becoming the moon's slave rather than her warrior. My father had told me many tales of how to avoid the moon's silvery glances, lest I failed her tests and became her slave.

The days of becoming a warrior to Shon had long passed, although I still had many dreams of earning the right to become such a warrior in my afterlife. But those dreams flickered wanly before my eyes now as the moon held my gaze. Her spirit was especially strong on this night. I tightened my grip on my dagger and prepared myself for the worst. My free hand was clutching a fistful of soil. I kept saliva gathered in my mouth, ready to spit if I needed to. I was prepared for anything.

'Look,' Iuzio said, when we reached the river.

I tried to look, but it was dark and I could see nothing but a vague shape that must have been my reflection. I knew, though, in many ways, what he was asking me to do. I knew of my people's obsession with reflections and how you could reach the Otherworld through your image in the water.

'This must be the place where your road begins, Ruk,' Iuzio said, as he stood beside me. 'And this must also be the place where your road ends.'

This didn't make any sense to me at all. And I told him so.

'Look at yourself again,' he said.' Tell me what you see.'

I looked hard, until my eyes crossed and everything blurred. But then my face seemed to become clear, although I didn't know how. It became so clear that it unnerved me, then it turned misty again. And at that moment, a woman's face appeared.

The face of Shon, I thought, our Lady's face come to enchant me. Or might this just be the face of the veiled woman on the western road?

Whoever she was, as I gazed into her eyes it almost seemed as though she was trying to drag me into her reflection. My hand was still on my dagger, but both my hands were now becoming clammy, so much so that the soil in my other hand was in danger of turning to mud. And all Iuzio did was smile.

I said, 'Why do you keep smiling, uncle?'

'What is a road, Ruk?' he returned, ignoring my question. 'Do you know what a road is? And what moves without moving? It will help you if you understand these riddles, Ruk.'

'But who is that woman in the water? Is she the spirit of the moon?'

As I spoke, I was looking at the great copper moon, now balancing on his right shoulder. The lady of the night was making eyes at me, luring me, weakening my legs. They were beginning to wobble.

'A road is less about distance, more about discovery,' Iuzio went on, ignoring my questions once again. 'Everyone is trying to find their way home, Ruk,' he added. 'Everyone is running in fear across the earth because they have forgotten where they are going. Remember that our Lady Moon will help you and guide you if you serve her in the right way, in the old way, as men and boys did in earlier times. But she will deny you that honour and play with your affections if you stray from your path. And then you will be in danger of straying onto Ana's path instead. You must not forget where you are going, not for one minute. You

125

must never stop understanding the road if you wish to help
our people. Do you wish to help our people?'

I nodded, adding, 'More than anything, uncle. But if
I am in England when my road ends, how can it be that my
journey will also end here? Because I will not be in England
when I begin. It doesn't make sense. England is so very far
away.'

'Is it?'

'Yes, it is.'

'How far is it?'

'I don't know. I cannot measure.'

'Where is England, Ruk?'

'I don't know. I already told you. England is west
somewhere. It is far away.'

I laughed, thinking this conversation was becoming
absurd and that Iuzio was starting to talk nonsense.

'What moves but does not move, Ruk?'

'I don't know.'

But then I thought a little. 'The road?' I asked,
expecting him to tell me that this was the wrong answer.

But he smiled, saying, 'You will need to answer *all*
the riddles if you are to complete your task. Follow me
now.'

We walked along the riverbank, Iuzio walking fast
while I ran behind, trying to keep up with him.

'Where are we going?' I called. I was imagining,
ridiculously, that we might just be going to England, so that
he could prove a point. And it would turn out that England
wasn't where I thought it was after all, but just beyond the
next field.

Suddenly we stopped, on the ridge of a great slope
that curved down into what appeared to be a wide dell. I had
been in this forest many times before, but had never come
across this great ditch. As I looked into it, it sang of
otherworldly fears and great enchantment. I thought I had
never seen such darkness collected all in one place before.

'You will need this,' Iuzio told me, suddenly
producing a sword in a scabbard and offering it to me.

126

As I took hold of it, I found it was very heavy and almost bigger than I was. I had never been given anything so large and so wonderful before.

'What?' I tried to say.

But he silenced me. 'Keep this by your side at all times,' he said. 'Do not let it out of your sight. Do not let anyone take it from you. And learn all you can about it. You are going to need it on your journey west. It will help with the answers to the riddles.'

I didn't know what to say. But I also kept peering down into the darkness that was lurking menacingly in front of me. Why had he brought me here? What was he trying to tell me? I could feel the darkness beginning to drag me into it, just by the very fact that it was there, just as the woman in the water had tried to drag me into her reflection when I had looked into her eyes. Perhaps Shon and the darkness are one and the same thing, I thought, remembering the terrible tests the moon's warriors were forced to undergo before they were worthy enough to champion her.

While I was peering into this great darkness, Iuzio said, 'Ask yourself this now, Ruk: Are you within Little Egypt or is Little Egypt within you? Is Ruk within England or is England within Ruk?'

Another riddle. People called our vast camp Little Egypt, mainly because it was the place that was inhabited by Egyptians. We had been settled in this place for a great many years, sometimes travelling away from it but always returning to it again, because it was a safe place to be. It would be strange to leave Little Egypt for good. Some wanted that, but others felt safe returning to the familiar great hillside. Now Iuzio's question made me think about leaving Little Egypt and never coming back.

Was I within Little Egypt or was Little Egypt within me? Was I within England or was England within me? These questions, these riddles... Why did we always need to have riddles?

My people had long had an obsession with riddles.

Elders sat around campfires for whole nights telling each other riddles, enjoying them in some strange way I could never understand. When you were initiated into adulthood, you were also initiated into the world of riddles. It was said that an Egyptian finally grew up whenever he got to understand and enjoy the nature of riddles. So I was doubting my own road to maturity more and more every time Iuzio gave me yet another riddle.

I stood scratching my head now, trying to understand what he had just said, asking myself what was within what, trying to remember his exact words.

What I really wanted was to examine the sword more closely by the light of my fire. It was so magnificent, I just couldn't stop looking at it.

But when I did finally look up I noticed that Iuzio had gone. I glanced around, looking for him, and as I did so I caught my foot on an exposed tree root and suddenly found myself falling head first down the slope, down and down, so far down that I imagined I was never going to stop falling. And all the while I was clutching the sword, ready to break my body rather than break my precious new weapon.

When I finally came to rest and tried to pull myself up, I found I couldn't move. My mouth had filled with earth and I was coughing and choking, unable to get my breath. I believed the soil had also got into my ears and my eyes, for my ears were full of silence and my eyes were full of darkness. And what was worse, hundreds of vines seemed to have entwined themselves around my legs and the lower half of my torso, and they weren't going to let me go.

I groaned. I didn't know if I was hurt because I couldn't move enough to test my limbs. The darkness was a thick black river oozing around me, pressing against me, pulling itself into different shapes that cut into my mind. Was there a dark tree in front of me? Or a tall man? Was that a tangle of gnarled branches over there? Or a gang of little people who had collected together to laugh and sneer at me?

Would Uncle Iuzio come to get me? He was taking

his time. Perhaps he had been a Locollico spirit after all, who had disguised himself so that he could push me over the ridge while my attention was held by the sword. I tried to call out to him, to see if he would answer, but my voice made no sound. And when I tried to reconstruct the words he had spoken, I couldn't remember them.

I was confused. Had I slipped down into the darker regions of the Lowerworld? And would the answer to one of the riddles free me? Or was I destined to end my life in this place, perhaps becoming a meal for the wild animals and monsters that roamed the Lowerworld at night. Was there a night in the Lowerworld? Was there a day? Did daylight ever reach this place? Were these dark regions about to claim my soul and transform it into a Locollico spirit?

I felt abandoned and betrayed. So I burst into tears. Like a baby I sobbed, calling for my mother. I wanted her to come and comfort me, to tell me this was just a dream. I wanted her to sing me songs, as she did when I was very tired or ill. I wanted her to step out of the darkness and tell me that I was safe and that everything was going to be alright.

I was lying with my arms wrapped tightly around the sword, clinging to it for all I was worth. But did I really want it? Warriorship was fine in stories, but did I want it in the real world? Perhaps I didn't any more. A sword couldn't put its arms around you and sing you to sleep in the way your mother could.

I kept my eyes closed, because whenever I opened them the darkness pulled itself into those terrifying shadowy forms and I didn't want to engage with any of them. I didn't know how I was ever going to get out of this place. Yes, I had a sword. I also had a good dagger. But what use were weapons if you couldn't move?

I went over the words that Uncle Iuzio had given me again, trying desperately to remember them. In our old tales the heroes and heroines repeatedly found their way out of difficult situations. They always found their way home. But I couldn't think of a single situation in any tale that was remotely comparable to this one. Nothing I had ever heard of had seemed as uncomfortable or terrifying as this.

Now I began to hear whispering voices coming out of the air. I had been afraid that this would happen. It was as if the darkness hadn't tormented me enough through my eyes. Now it had to torment me through my ears too.

To combat the whispering I tried to sing some comforting songs to myself. And to my surprise I suddenly remembered the words of the riddle. Perhaps I'd been frightened into remembering them. It didn't matter. I was elated as they came rushing back to me. It was as if they were being spoken by Uncle Iuzio himself: 'Ask yourself, Ruk, are you within Little Egypt or is Little Egypt within you? Is Ruk within England or is England within Ruk? This must be the place where your road begins, Ruk. And this must also be the place where your road ends.'

I could remember all these words now plainly. But I also remembered making a promise to travel to England to curse and kill a man. So my predicament was probably my just reward and no amount of magical riddles would be powerful enough to save me.

I began crying again, tears streaming down my face and bringing the strong taste of salt as they trickled into my open mouth. All my dreams of being a warrior, all my hopes of leading my people to the western horizon and the land called England were being swallowed by the darkness. I was a failure, a fool and a coward. And I deserved to be exactly where I was.

But the words kept coming. Now I was hearing the voice of a woman, sweet and haunting, saying, 'What needs to be beloved and true and hateful and venomous all at the same time, Ruk?'

'Ana!' I thought. This must be the voice of the beautiful forest queen who became Beng's wife.

I heard it again: 'When is a sword not a sword?'

Slowly, very slowly, I decided to open my eyes, one at a time, first to a narrow slit, ready to close them again quickly if I needed to.

Through the narrow slits I saw the shape of a woman forming, the same woman I had seen in the water. I was seeing her more clearly this time. She was extremely beautiful, with big dark smiling eyes, and was covered in colourful veils and coins. I knew she was a spirit because I could see right through her: the branch of a tree cut diagonally down her body and leaves fluttered both across and through her face. I did not flinch, but bravely kept both my eyes upon her as she floated about in front of me, sometimes bending over to touch me with a warm soft hand.

'Please don't hurt me,' I begged, tearful again, just in case she was Ana after all.

She widened her eyes. 'I think you would be capable of doing much more damage than I could ever do, Ruk,' she said, quite amused. 'You are, after all, the one who has the sword.'

She was right. I was still clutching the sword tightly.

'A spirit cannot be killed by the sword,' I reminded her.

'No, Ruk. But a sword can be killed by the spirit.'

She saw my puzzled expression and added, 'Think about it. It is something you will be called upon to learn.'

'Can it?' I asked. 'Can a sword be killed by the spirit?'

'Listen to me,' she said, 'and think about my riddle. What needs to be beloved and true and hateful and venomous all at the same time? If you answer this riddle, Ruk, you will understand your sword. And if you understand your sword, you will be able to answer the other riddle and release yourself from this place.'

I thought about it. 'A man who is being attacked,' I said, pondering on the words, 'a man who is being attacked, yes, because he will need to love his own cause and fight for his own cause at the same time.'

As I spoke, the sword seemed to be giving me a new but very strange kind of inner strength.

'Yes,' I said, thinking out loud. 'I think this is the

answer, auntie: a man with a cause, because a man with a cause is powerless without his sword.'

She smiled. She had such a beautiful smile.

'So the answer to that riddle is a sword?' I asked.

She nodded. 'A sword needs to be beloved and true and hateful and venomous all at the same time,' she said, 'otherwise it cannot serve its master. Remember, Ruk, that you must never lose your fight. A warrior is a mixture of many things, which he learns to manage very skilfully. You must never lose the memory of that which can cut people down, nor the memory of that which can bring people help and comfort. Managing these two emotions is difficult, but a successful warrior is able to do it well. Keep these memories alive inside, Ruk, and you will preserve the strong bond there is between love and hate.'

'I understand,' I told her. 'But you said the sword can be killed by the spirit, auntie.' I still wanted to understand what she meant by this.

'Think about it, Ruk,' she said. 'Think about it in the light of what I have just told you.'

'Are you the spirit of the moon?' I asked.

Like Iuzio, she ignored my question. Ancestors always ignored your questions when they didn't want to answer them. But I really wanted to know who she was.

'Are you an ancestor of mine, auntie?'

'Answer the next riddle,' she said, 'then I will tell you. When is a sword not a sword, Ruk?'

'If you are an ancestor,' I said, disregarding the riddle entirely, 'I think you must be the most beautiful ancestor that ever was. You are a beautiful ancestor come to lure me to fight for you on an eternal battlefield.'

I was babbling, but it seemed so romantic and chivalrous and yet terrible at the same time – fighting an eternal battle for our ancestral line, fighting for a lady as gracious as the moon. And yet it attracted me, stirring great feelings of passion inside. And I might even be addressing the moon herself.

'Answer my riddle,' she was insisting now, touching

my arm with soft warm fingers.

I was thinking about it, but I was so enchanted by her I started to feel myself slipping away again, slipping down into the darkness. Perhaps it was the darkness itself doing the enchanting.

'Ruk!' the lady said loudly in my ear. 'You must answer the riddle now! When is a sword not a sword? When is a sword not a sword? When is a sword not a sword?'

She would not let me slip away. I opened my eyes wide and saw her very clearly: her long dark hair bearing silver coins, a thick gold ring ballooning out of her nostril. I could smell the scent of her and as I reached out and touched her she felt warm and fleshy and comforting. I felt safe in her presence and scared of her at the same time. And soon I saw that Uncle Iuzio had come to join her. He too seemed real as I reached out and touched him. His eyes were intensely blue; his hair was flaming red. I wanted to look at both of them more closely and study them for a long time, but the darkness was engulfing me once more.

Then I was swimming about on a battlefield where I was riding a white horse and where the lady was riding behind me with her arms locked tightly around my waist. I was certain she was an ancestor now and not the spirit of the moon. I felt sure she was an ancient grandmother of mine, the one my people talked about and revered. And we were riding up into the sky, through the clouds, both of us free at last as we rode into a mist that seemed to take all my pain and fear away. There were no other warriors galloping alongside us, but I somehow knew that this place was where great warriors lived, perhaps the place where they found their courage.

Was I dying and rising up into the heavens to become an ancestor like the one who was riding behind me? Perhaps this wasn't a battlefield after all, but an ancestral realm where I was destined to spend the rest of eternity, after dying in the ditch.

My horse was moving swiftly; my new sword, gleaming silver, was firmly in my hand. I didn't know where we were going, but we seemed to be cantering about all over the place and it felt exhilarating and calming at the same time, because the mist took us this way and that, but really no way at all. And it drifted into my eyes and ears, as if reassuring me that all was well.

But then, up ahead, I caught sight of something white, something gleaming. It looked like a great stone, standing freely on its own. Was it a stone? A stone standing there in the sky?

Stones could talk, I remembered. If you touched them you could ask them questions and they would give you wise answers. If I walked up and touched this stone perhaps I could learn everything I had ever wanted to know.

I brought my horse to a halt, clambered down and approached the stone, respectfully bowing my head as I moved closer.

And only when I was standing in front of it did I realise that this was no simple stone but a gigantic cross, stretching way above me and way below.

Yes, Chi, when I looked up I wasn't able to see the pinnacle of this colossal monument, nor could I see its base, which seemed to descend into the depths of the earth. There was an eerie silence, a warning perhaps to turn away. But I was much too curious. And I didn't want to let an opportunity to touch such a great stone pass me by. I thought that the knowledge it would bring me would give me everything I needed.

But how was this incredible monument able to stand on its own in the sky like this? Wasn't it a miracle?

I soon began to realise that I too must be balancing in the sky, because there was nothing under my feet. I glanced down, but I didn't fall. And then I jumped, but I didn't fall. I should have been falling, but I wasn't falling.

I wanted to show my lady ancestor what I had found, but when I turned and looked for her, both she and the horse had disappeared into the mist. And the mist now had a purply hue to it, as though someone was shining a light through it from somewhere beyond.

'Who's there?' I asked.

No answer came, but then the source of the light became apparent as a figure stepped towards me: a woman, beautiful, swathed in purple from head to toe and radiating light. She was tall, broad and strong, and the gently billowing purple veils that covered her whole body fell behind her in a great train.

I blinked and rubbed my eyes. Was I really seeing this incredible sight? Yes, I was. And I knew also that this was the alluring veiled woman upon my western road, the one who had beckoned me to join her so often when I had been lying beside the campfire.

I went down on one knee, without further question, bowing my head to her.

'My lady,' I said humbly.

As she reached me, she raised me up.

And when she looked into my eyes with her own dark eyes, shimmering through her purple veil, I found myself swimming about all over again, drowning in her beauty. This woman was capturing my heart.

I wanted to ask who she was, but no words would pass my lips. I was being mesmerised by all that blinding purple.

'Are you ready for the great western road now?' she asked.

I found it hard to speak, but managed to mumble a faint 'yes'.

'Are you ready to champion me?'

Again a faint 'yes'.

'This is the great western road, Ruk,' she told me, holding out her arm in the direction of the stone that had become the cross.

I looked up at the cross and saw that it was changing shape once again. The cold hard stone seemed to have melted and it was now, unbelievably, a long road snaking away into the mist.

'The western road,' I mumbled, 'is this really the western road?'

'It is a road that will lead you anywhere you wish to go,' the woman said.

'But I only want to go west.'

'All roads will lead you astray before they take you to your destination, Ruk.'

'The road that brings you always carries you away,' I mumbled. Yes, this was all making sense now.

'Who are you?' I finally managed to ask.

'You know who I am,' she said. 'Haven't I been visiting you long enough? It is time now to call to your side all those people who wish to return to their home in the west. Now is the time to lead them home, Ruk.'

I stared at her. I couldn't believe she was speaking to me in this way after all this time.

She had turned to look behind us and there I saw shapes floating about in the purple mist, the vague shapes of people.

'Those are the people,' she said.

They were strange people, mere grey shapes, all of them drifting, floating towards me through the air.

'Who are they?' I wanted to know, but the veiled woman did not answer.

The purple mist was beginning to thicken all around me now, moving in and out of my eyes, ears and mouth. And I couldn't take my eyes off the road for a moment, for we were all caught upon some strange beam that seemed to be trying to draw us all closer to it.

'Call them, Ruk, call them,' the spirit woman said. 'Don't let them go. For I can do nothing unless you help me. You want to help me, don't you? I need someone to protect me. A road has no arms and no legs and cannot carry anyone anywhere without help. I need a warrior to help me, Ruk, someone to help me carry all those who wish to travel to the west.'

She was standing close to me and I could feel an attraction for her beginning to rise within me.

'Why do you hesitate, Ruk? Why do you hesitate?'

I was hesitating because as well as watching the road,

I was also watching the floating people, most of whom were just drifting aimlessly, bumping into each other and sometimes bumping into me. And it was becoming apparent that most of the grey figures were lifeless.

'Are these people dead?' I asked, horrified. 'Am I standing in an otherworldly graveyard of lost souls?'

The spirit laughed. 'Do not fear, Ruk,' she said. 'These people are merely looking for the western road, which is here in front of them. They are looking for a leader. And all you have to do is touch the stone with your sword, fearlessly. Just touch it, Ruk, and you'll acquire great knowledge and will become everything you have ever wanted to be. Do not fear, do not fear.'

Touch the stone? I looked back at the road and she was right – it had once again become a great stone.

'But which is it really?' I asked in some confusion. 'It keeps changing. Is it a road, a cross or a stone?'

'It can be anything you want it to be,' she said. 'The power of stone is complete and can transform into anything at all, because it is magical, Ruk. And it can give you anything you desire, including me.'

Passion rose uncontrollably within me as she spoke these words. It was true that here was everything I had ever wanted: the western road, great knowledge and a most beautiful woman.

She was offering me a cup. 'We will drink to your new life, Ruk, to our new life together. Just touch the stone with the tip of your sword. Have no fear and all will be well. Touch it, Ruk. Touch it.'

I stretched out my sword, with a shaking hand.

'No, you are not relaxed enough,' she said.

I was still afraid. I watched as the stone became the road again, almost making contact with it with the silver tip of the blade. But it wasn't always a road, was it? It was also a stone, and sometimes a cross, and probably many other things as well. I discovered that whenever I withdrew my sword, it became a stone. And if I brought my sword closer, it became a road. But sometimes the cross reappeared. I was very confused. And my fear had a hand in it all. My fear was in fact helping me to see things as they were.

And something was telling me not to touch anything at all – perhaps my lady ancestor, perhaps Iuzio, perhaps plain common sense. My sword was almost upon the road. But something seemed to be trying to pull my hand away.

And suddenly I knew I had to honour that, and when I finally gave in to my fear and stepped away, I had the greatest shock of all as I realised that there was actually nothing in front of me at all: no stone, no woman, just empty space.

My heart was beating fast. A bitter taste was in my mouth. I was more scared than I had ever been. And yet I was suddenly able to see what was going on. And I was grateful for that.

'Answer the riddles, Ruk,' I then heard my lady ancestor say loudly in my ear. My fear seemed to bring her voice closer. 'You must answer all the riddles now if you wish to learn what is going on here and the difference between a shadow road and a true road. You must answer the riddles if you want to become a true warrior.'

I stood gazing at the grey lifeless people who were drifting past me. They seemed real enough as they floated by, sometimes even holding onto my clothes. I did not like their faces, for whenever any of them came close I saw that they had great grey sunken eyes: the eyes of death. And all of them had bony grasping fingers, fingers that might sink into my flesh were I to allow them to touch me for too long.

Floating on, they seemed to disappear into the emptiness where the stone had been. So the stone had been a shape made up of people. And the cross had been a shape made up of people. And the western road had been a shape made up of people: people forming the shapes of things.

People – or shadows, Chi?

And I asked, and still ask, how many things are there in the world that are not things at all, but shapes made up of shadows? Yes.

And how could this beautiful veiled woman have been a part of all this? Is this what beautiful women did? Perhaps, after all, she was one of the many children of Beng and Ana, a Locollico daughter.

This was trickery, an otherwordly game of Akahna. And I wanted none of it.

So I lifted my sword and slashed at the air, slashing and slashing madly. I did not want to become a shadow, even though the veiled woman had attracted me so very much. I did not want to lose my soul for any woman. I wanted only what was real.

But then there came a crawling sensation on my skin, as though a great insect were upon me. But when I looked there was nothing there. I danced about, shrieking, trying to brush the invisible insect away. The sensation of many tiny legs crawling upon me was more than I could bear. The veiled woman had vanished and I knew she was something to do with the insect. I shouted and slashed and shouted and slashed. I loved her no more.

'When is a sword not a sword, Ruk? When is a sword not a sword? When is a sword not a sword?'

I lost my balance and began to plummet, falling down and down from the sky. And I soon became aware of lying in the wood once again, shivering badly with the cold and with the creeping sensation all over my skin. I was lying upon something damp. A puddle? A marshy bog in the ground? The earth seemed to have shifted below me, causing the top half of my body to have slipped below the bottom half. My legs were sticking up above me, making me feel intensely uncomfortable. I still couldn't move. And I was shivering and shivering. And the feeling of insects on my skin was driving me mad.

The sword was still in my arms, held tight against my chest, but as I started to lose consciousness, it seemed to be moving of its own accord. Was it leaving my arms? Was the veiled woman back again? No, she had gone. The crawling sensation had lessened. But it felt as if my sword was moving.

Then I caught sight of a hooded figure, faint against the thick darkness, and this figure, with spidery but gentle fingers, seemed to be trying to ease my sword out of my arms. Was this the source of the insect feelings – these spidery fingers touching me?

The hooded figure was gentle. He wasn't trying to grab my sword so that he could run off with it. He was merely attempting to ease the weapon out of my arms, as if easing a burden from me. And in fact, the more I lost consciousness, the more it felt as though I had actually asked him to take it from me.

Had I? And who was he? Another shadow?

I tried to keep my eyes open and again tried singing so that I could remain alert. I was still shivering badly and now also sweating sometimes, the sweat forming a thick sticky syrup on my skin. The dampness beneath my body seemed to be seeping into my bones and I knew I was developing a fever. The hooded figure continued to hover around me like some wild animal stalking its prey. He would disappear and reappear, disappear and reappear over and over again, watching and waiting for me to slip completely away so that he might move in on me and steal my sword. His large hood had been pulled right down over his face, but I had the strange feeling that were it to be pushed back, he would have no face at all.

'Who are you?' I tried asking.

He did not answer.

'What do you want?' I asked, although I knew full well what he was after.

Again he did not answer me.

'Are you a spirit?' I demanded.

I could not get him to speak to me, no matter how much I tried.

The forest spirits, I thought then, I must ask the forest spirits to come to my aid. I must call for the Bari Weshen Dai, our Great Forest Mother. She helped all children who ran into trouble in the forest. Was I a child in need? Or was I a man who could not find his courage? I didn't know. Perhaps I was neither. Perhaps I was caught upon that bridge between childhood and manhood. My elders seemed to think we all entered such a place when we reached the phase of life called Jal Raht. And when we were in this place, we were forced to find the strength that we would be able to call upon in later life. If we did not find that strength then, we might never find it. We might never grow up.

But if this was what adulthood was all about, I didn't know if I wanted it. Did I want to spend all this time with shadows who lured me and then tricked me and who simply hung around trying, oh so nicely, to steal my sword?

'Bari Weshen Dai!' I cried, tears once again beginning to stream down my face. 'Help me! Please help me.'

I had called for the Bari Weshen Dai once before when I had been lost in the forest. I had been small then and she had come to my aid straightaway. It had been raining and the raindrops dripping down from the branches had collected together and formed the shape of a fair-skinned motherly woman who had bent over me and held my hand.

'Let's take you home, Ruk,' she had said, and holding my hand, she had escorted me back to my camp and then disappeared.

'Who brought you home?' my family asked.

'A lady,' I told them, describing how fair she was and the woodland scent she had exuded.

'The Bari Weshen Dai,' my grandmother announced, 'our most gracious Forest Mother.'

She did not spit at all that time, but smiled and gave me something nice to eat.

The Bari Weshen Dai might have come to my aid then, but she was not coming now, and that told me that I was entering the realm of manhood whether I liked it or not.

What was I to do? The fever was worsening. And I was becoming irritable and angry, angry that this hooded spirit should spoil my Jal Raht. Was that, after all, what he was really trying to steal from me?

It would have been so easy to relinquish my sword. He wasn't fighting me for it. In fact he was being extremely polite about it all, as though he was doing me a service by relieving me of it. He persistently bowed his head and opened his palms in humbleness.

But I was still angry.

'No!' I cried out, with sudden strength. 'No! No! Go away. You won't take my sword!'

I heard my own voice echoing in the darkness up above me, down below me and all around me. And that seemed to empower me.

'When is a sword not a sword, Ruk?' I heard a quick voice speaking at my ear. It seemed that whenever I chose to take command, the voice of my lady ancestor returned. Now she was hovering directly in front me. I could see every part of her face clearly.

But I was still crying, 'No!'

Her voice became louder and even more urgent: 'Ruk, answer the riddle. Answer it *now*! When is a sword not a sword?'

The groping fingers of the hooded figure were back again and the spirit was again easing the sword out of my arms, silently, humbly and politely.

I saw desperation in the eyes of my beautiful ancestor. And I knew this time I had to do something.

But still I cried, 'No! No! No!', my anger surging up again and again within me.

'Think, Ruk, *think*,' she insisted.

And then as I looked at the hooded figure I suddenly had the answer, because I saw whenever the sword was in my own hands it remained a sword, but whenever it passed into his hands, it started changing into a cross.

Was it true that such a beautiful shiny sword could also become a dark ugly cross?

Was my sword about to become a shadow sword?

A spirit cannot be killed by the sword, but a sword

142

can be killed by the spirit, I also recalled.

And I saw that whenever the sword left my hands its passion diminished, its spirit started to bleed and it started to become a shadow. And I knew that this would also start happening to me. No life would remain within me should the blood leave my body. I would become pure shadow in a matter of minutes, perhaps seconds. Unless I took some kind of action I would be destined for a life in the Shadow Lands, where my body would walk the earth filled not with my own spirit, but with a great many shadows.

As if it was aware of what I was thinking, the spirit grasped my sword more firmly, then meekly moved away with it in his arms. He did not walk; he drifted, he shifted, he eased himself along.

'No!' I shouted.

And with renewed strength I took my dagger and hacked at the vines that were still entwined around my legs, pulling at them urgently until I had cut myself free.

And then I got up and followed the spirit down, down, deep into the bottomless regions of the ditch. Stumbling, I slid down after him, fear pressing into me, until we entered a cave, lit at the centre by a strange purply light.

The spirit took my sword to the centre of the cave and laid it down carefully on an altar. I knew what was going to happen: there would be a sacrifice, a sacrifice of a part of me. It was as if my own body, my own soul, were being laid out upon the altar. And soon I was seeing other hooded figures joining the dark spirit at the altar, all of them with great hoods over their faceless faces, all of them drifting, shifting, creeping, easing themselves along.

And then I saw that the hilt of the sword was no longer a hilt and the blade was no longer a blade. The fight in my sword had gone. The spirit in my sword was being bled away. And the hooded figure was lifting the sword high and it was changing, changing into something it wasn't, just as the stone had done, and just as I was doing as I watched.

But did it matter that everything was changing in this way? Did it really matter?

As I watched my sword becoming a tall silver cross, a smaller version of the one I had seen in the sky, I felt myself being sucked in, just as the grey lifeless people had been sucked in, and yet it didn't seem to matter. My sword had gone, but I would never need to fight again. Why should I fight? I didn't need to. I didn't need to feel the heat of courage and passion. I didn't need to feel responsible any more. I didn't need to be a warrior.

I could feel my spirit being drained away. And I sank down onto the cave floor, weakening, sweating, burning up with fever.

But as I looked at the cross, I saw that beneath its silver skin there lurked a dark venom, oozing green slime and giving off a foul odour. And I felt my wild and free spirit oozing out of me, just as the slime was oozing out of the cross. And I knew that Beng would feed off my soul, just as he would feed off the many souls he was trying to draw in through these shadow monks who were his servants.

And one great realisation came to me in that cave, Chi: that there, in that place, within my Jal Raht, I was witnessing the makings of a way of life that was destined to change the world.

* * * * *

Yes, Chi, as terrible as that experience was, it helped me to understand the way of life that would draw the spirit of the wild from the souls of people in many places throughout the world.

Religion, in its many forms, would change the face of the earth irreparably.

The west was doomed. I knew the west was destined to bear the brunt of the dark cloud that Beng was in the throes of draping across this ancient land and its native peoples. I saw a dark menacing cloud gathering in the east, vile and terrible at its centre, and drifting to the west, and all who were touched by it fell into a great slumber, from which some never recovered.

144

And the Bari Weshen Dai lay sleeping, the Great Forest Mother enchanted. It would take a spell of a very special kind to wake her. For this spell had been designed to be unbreakable.

'Why?' I thought. 'Why should this happen? Why would any spirit want to wreak such havoc upon the world? What could be gained from it?'

These were questions I knew I would want to ask Iuzio at a later time.

But there on that cave floor, I knew that the warrior in me had to come to life.

So I rose up, staggering about and shouting at the top of my voice. I ran into the centre of the cave, rushing at all the bloodless hooded figures, and grabbed hold of my sword, catching it by its blade.

That blade had already blunted, for I found I could take hold of it quite firmly and pull it out of the monk's hands without being harmed. Yes, although the blade was firmly in both my hands, it drew no blood, because the blood of its spirit and the blood of my spirit had already begun to depart. I knew I could try to sharpen it here in this place, but its edge would never return. I knew I could try to stab someone here in this place, but blood would never be spilled. For this was the very heartland of the bloodless, the land of the walking dead, a realm within the Shadow World.

And these shadows were clearly not human. Perhaps they had once been so, long ago. Perhaps they were men who had also been in the position I was in now and who had failed their Jal Raht. But now they were but an illusion, mere fragments of nothingness. I held my sword by its hilt, swinging it round above my head, slicing through all of them one by one, over and over again.

But it seemed I was wasting my energy, because they had no blood and no flesh and could not be harmed. They kept coming towards me, tirelessly bowing and reaching out for my sword, fingering my clothes with their cold, bony, creeping hands. No matter how much I cut into them, I just couldn't seem to hurt them.

And yet my anger did not lessen. And it was at that point that I knew that I was reclaiming my soul, my courage and the power in my sword. My fight was returning to me, together with my blood. And I then saw all the shadows starting to shrink away, meekly and silently creeping back into their shadow world. And I came out of the cave and made my way back up the slope, slipping and stumbling, panting and shaking as I went.

And only then did my hands begin to hurt. They hurt so badly that I cried out in agony. By the time I reached the top of the ditch, blood was dripping from them. And I realised I still had my blood after all.

I licked my hands. I wanted to taste my own blood, because it meant that I was alive again. And I knew that my sword was a sword and the hilt was a hilt and the blade was a blade. And life was in the land of the living, in the natural Middleworld, which was the only land I ever wanted to be in.

And as I made my way back to my flickering campfire I fell on the ground.

And I heard: 'This must be where your road begins, Ruk. And this must also be where your road ends.'

And I pulled a blanket over myself and hugged my sword and cried because I understood. I understood at last.

A sword was not a sword when it became a cross. And because I understood fear I understood courage. I understood the warrior. And I knew that I would begin my journey west as a warrior and end my journey west as a warrior. I would begin my journey from the strong place I had found within myself and I would end my journey in the same place. That place was the realm of the warrior.

And I knew I would never leave that place, no matter what I did, no matter where I went. And I would fight for the true spirit of our people and for the ancient blood memory of all those who had souls. I would not allow life to leave me ever again.

Oh, Chi, it was such a realisation to know that I would begin and end my journey there, exactly where I was, within the life I had inside me, that I cried for a very long time.

I had learned a great lesson: that the great battle to survive is in us all. And, Chi, I knew that this would always be the greatest battle of a person's life.

* * * * *

I did not look at the monks in the same way after I had travelled into the darkness of the Lowerworld. And I did not look at women in the same way after I had travelled into the brightness of the Upperworld. I did not look at my people in the same way after I had seen what life was really all about.

I have scars now on both my hands, across the middle of my palms. My elders say they are lucky because they were made by the sword that Iuzio gave me and because they were made during my first real initiation into being a man. They are also lucky because they add a strong line to my palms which other people don't have. And all those who read palms in my tribe say that this is one of the luckiest signs there is. And I am truly blessed.

After my battle with the hooded shadows, who I afterwards learned were Locollico spirits who had long been hunting my soul, I had a lot to think about.

On that first morning when dawn greeted me, I cried all over again, for I never thought I would see a dawn again. I was so glad to see the sun and the daylight, so glad to be alive.

And as I rolled over, yawning, I became aware that both of my hands had been bound with something soothing. And I had been tucked up snugly inside a blanket, with my sword safely by my side.

Someone near to me was throwing wood onto my fire, which was burning unusually brightly. I sat up and blinked.

'Iuzio?'

But it wasn't Iuzio. It was a child, a boy. Or was it?

147

'Would you like some water?' he asked.

I blinked again. He was sitting near me, dressed in peajamangris, grey tunic and white leggings. He was holding my cup out to me and had red wool tied around his wrists and neck. But as I adjusted my eyes a little more I realised that there was something different, something odd about him.

I had thought he was sitting down when really he was standing up. He was short, much shorter than the average boy normally was. And I instinctively found myself scrambling to get up so that I could throw some protective soil over myself and move away from him.

Then I realised that I had brought back with me from the Lowerworld one of the woodland spirits, one of the small folk. I was sharing my campfire with a member of the Keshali race, a race of magical beings from the Otherworld.

'Do you want this water or don't you?' he asked, abruptly, still holding the cup out to me and probably wondering what I was doing wrestling with my blanket, which had entwined itself tightly round me. His dark eyes were full of mischief, as Keshali eyes were, blinking at me above the cup.

I pulled an arm out of the blanket and took the water, sipping it slowly and not unapologetically. The Keshali were benevolent spirits, but many also had a strong will and enduring magical power, and if you knew what was good for you, you stayed on the right side of them.

'Are you one of the little folk from beneath the earth?' I asked bravely, knowing I might as well hear the truth now as later.

'What do you think?' he came back, grinning.

I looked him up and down again and couldn't decide what he was, and then I sat back on my elbows, feeling suddenly weak. I looked at my hands. They had been bound in a very caring way with some kind of material and treated with a herbal mixture, and both were feeling very stiff.

'You injured yourself,' the boy told me. 'I found

148

you at the top of the slope over there, groaning, so I dragged you back over here, which was difficult, because you were so heavy. But then you were speaking with the tongues of spirits which I didn't like, so I kept you warm, threw salt all over you and told the spirits to go away. And it looks like they did.'

'Thank you.'

'Are you warm enough?'

'Yes, thank you.'

'I will have to teach you some tricks, then you won't be led astray by that slow wit of yours.'

'My wit isn't slow.'

He pulled a face.

'Why are you here with me?' I asked.

He shrugged, then said, 'Because we need to get to know each other.'

'Are you a friend of Iuzio's?'

'Who?'

'Are you a friend of Shon's?'

He frowned.

'Are you a friend of any of my ancestors?'

He blinked at me, then said, 'You've been to the Lowerworld, my friend, haven't you? They dragged you down there, didn't they?'

'They didn't drag me,' I told him, coolly. 'I went by myself.'

He laughed out loud. 'No one goes by themselves to the Lowerworld to meet shadows, not unless they're stupid.'

I ignored this and lay back again, studying my hands one after the other. He had bandaged them up very skilfully.

'So I had a difficult time in the Lowerworld. But you still haven't answered my question. Why are you here with me?' I said.

'I'm here to help you. I saw you needed help and I gave you help,' he shrugged.

'And I am most grateful for it. But I will need to return to my camp now.'

'Yes,' he said. 'I know. And I will come with you.'

'Come with me?'

'That's what I said, didn't I?'

'Why do you need to come with me? Am I bound to you now forever? Do I have to serve you for the rest of my days?'

He thought about this for a while, then laughed. 'We will be spending a lot of time together, you and I,' he said. 'You're going to need my advice. So we might as well get to know each other.'

I didn't understand. All I could think was that perhaps I had received a curse on my travels down in the Lowerworld. Perhaps I was destined to spend the rest of my life with this little man at my side, someone no one else in the world would ever be able to see.

'But don't you live here in the forest?' I asked.

'Sometimes,' he answered.

'Sometimes? But...'

'But what?' he said, knitting his brows in agitation, putting his small fists on his small hips and looking at me impatiently. Then he sighed. 'Don't I remind you of anyone, fool?'

I was about to tell him that I wasn't a fool when he turned his back on me. And only then did I realise what he was showing me and where I had seen him before.

As he turned around to face me, I announced: 'The thief in the church!'

He grinned.

'But you're small. You're not a normal boy. And you're not a normal man either. '

'And which one are you then? A normal boy or a normal man?'

I knew what he was referring to. I fell silent.

'No normal boy *or* man would go whistling down to the Lowerworld,' he went on, 'not on his own.'

I gave in and apologised.

He was, in fact, an ordinary boy, a little older than myself it seemed, but smaller in stature than one of his age.

'I am Diverous,' he announced with pride, giving me a sweeping bow. 'And I am proud to be small and to have ancestors who are indeed woodland folk and who live in the magical Otherworld and who have great power.

'So, you are right, fool, about my origins. Fools can learn a lot from me, Ruk, as indeed you can. First, though, my friend, you will have to think more quickly if you want to play the game of Akahna better than you played it in the church, or others will reach all the spoils before you do, as I was able to. Do not be fooled by my size. I have been playing the game of Akahna for a good many years now. And I have even played it in the Otherworld with my kind, the woodland folk, for that is where the game was born.' He paused to grin at me again. 'Know, fool, that we shall become brothers when we are all travelling to England together, because my father told me –'

'Your father?' I cried. 'Who is your father?'

He started laughing. 'You didn't know that my father was Hawk, did you? He isn't my real father, of course. My real father is a member of a small band of Keshali who live in the forest here. But Hawk felt sorry for me and adopted me. And because he made a mistress out of my mother – who, by the way, is of this world – he felt obliged to protect me. And that was for his own good, you see, because of my strong magical powers. Oh, don't look so surprised. My father told me all about you, so I know much more about you than you think. I am half-Egyptian, you know, fool.'

I was both amused and offended at what he had to say, amused at his story because he and Uncle Hawk seemed so remote from each other that the situation was laughable, but also offended at his persistence in addressing me as 'fool'.

However, a lot began slotting into place. I realised Uncle Hawk had sent his tracker son to find me because he wanted to know where I was. He wanted to ensure that I wasn't going to run away. He wasn't going to let me change my mind about the journey to England. My fate was sealed. There was no going back.

I felt as though I had already fought, and won, the biggest battle of my entire life. The fact that another battle lay just around the corner was hard to take in.

We put out the fire and walked back to my camp, Div taking small steps while I walked slowly, carrying my sword in my arms.

Div talked a lot. I had heard from my elders that Keshali folk talked a lot.

'I am a half-breed because my mother mated with a member of the Keshali race when she was enchanted to walk beneath the earth,' he explained boastfully. 'There are very few like me anywhere in the normal world.'

'Do you really have great magical power?' I had to ask.

He laughed. 'I helped pull you up out of the Lowerworld, didn't I?'

'I thought I came up by myself.'

'Not quite.'

'So how did you pull me out then?'

'It is a secret. I used a special power known only to my true father's race.'

I laughed and pretended to believe him. But he believed my own story of the adventures I'd had down in the Lowerworld with the hooded figures and in the Upperworld with the veiled woman.

'My sword will be very important to me now,' I assured him. 'It has become the most important thing in my life.'

'Sword?' he asked.

'Yes,' I said, holding it up to show to him with a little difficulty as I transferred it from my arms to my hands. It was heavy and my hands were still painful.

He stopped and looked at one of my hands, then took hold of my wrist, twisting and turning it, which made me yelp. He scratched his head.

'I see no sword, Ruk,' he announced. 'Did you take a knock on the head?'

I frowned. 'What are you talking about? Look, I'm showing you my sword. It's right here in front of your nose.'

'But there is no sword, Ruk. Really, there's nothing there.'

I held the sword right in front of him, vertically, horizontally, in every way possible, but still he couldn't see it.

I thought he was teasing me, or that he was envious and didn't want to acknowledge what I had been given, but he was adamant.

'Ruk, I promise you, I see no sword in your hands.'

'But you saw the cuts it made when you bandaged my hands,' I protested.

'Of course I saw cuts. And there is no doubt that they were made by a sword. But I don't see any sword now,' he insisted, and walked on, shaking his head and mumbling to himself.

'You told me you were a magical being,' I yelled after him. 'If that's so, why can't you see my sword?'

He stopped walking and turned to look at me, saying, 'Because it is born of a magic that is beyond me, fool.'

Then he walked away again and I looked down at my hands once more, at the beautiful sword lying between them. 'A magic that is beyond him,' I thought. 'Could it be a magic that is beyond anyone?'

I was eager to get back to camp to show others my sword, but there too it proved to be a source of confusion. For as I related the story of what had happened to me in the forest, no one commented on the shiny weapon I was lovingly cradling in my arms.

Clearly, no one was able to see it.

But when I was alone with my grandmother I only had to say 'Iuzio' and she cooed in delight, a tear filling her eye.

She told me I had been chosen by Iuzio to step into the Long Reflection and I had also had the good fortune to meet one of my ancient grandmothers. And that meant that my own spirit would now walk a divine road, collecting up the wisdom from those who were behind me and passing it on to those who were ahead. That was my task now, that was my new responsibility, and that would turn me into a real man. And I had to remember not to let my people down.

'The road that brings you always carries you away,' I sat there thinking. 'The river that brings your reflection always carries it away.'

In the camp there was great excitement. I would become a warrior, they said. I would lead my people to England and a step closer to the Otherworld. By my hand, our people would have a chance to preserve our ancient knowledge and return to their ancestral homeland. Even though I was young and the task was great, they said, I was equipped to carry it out. I would find a way.

But I was troubled. For still no one could see my sword. 'What sword?' they kept asking whenever I mentioned it, whenever I tried to show it to them. No one could see it except the one who had given it to me. Iuzio always smiled with delight when he saw my sword in my hand.

'You have been given this sacred object to help you through your journey in life,' he told me later. 'Each of the seven who step into the Long Reflection will receive a gift which can be passed down to Chi in the future, to help the Great Ancestral Chain survive and to banish the curse that has been laid upon this land.'

* * * * *

I told you that I stand tall, taller than the rambling hedgerow but smaller than the sky. I told you I snake my way deep down into the earth but that I also fly high in the wind. And I told you I have the power to spread my seed, the power to die, and that I have a warm brown solid body and a spirit that is older than anything you will ever find.

154

Well, you would think that as a warrior I would have received a warrior's name. But Ruslo Ruk, or Oak, remained my name my whole life long. The riddle, Chi, tells you what I am.

My elders link trees with courage and oaks with warriors. Oaks stand their ground, they say. Oaks do not turn and run. Oaks have the sturdiest, strongest spirits. And if a warrior needed something to make him strong, he would stand beside an oak with his palm spread against it, or better still, his back up against it. He would then absorb something of that magnificent tree's spirit, providing he was worthy enough. And he would never run from his foes.

But if anyone ever needed the help of the oak, I did. For as I grew older, I realised just how strong a man needed to be for his spirit to come even remotely close to the spirit of this magnificent tree.

My name changed several times, not least because I *was* the fool Div always said I was. Sometimes my people called me Cowardly Ruk, or Witless Ruk, or Sleeping Ruk, and Div, who stayed with me and became a true friend, called me many more names whenever I had occasion to slip out of my warrior role. Knowing the oaks well because of his Keshali blood, he would not allow me to slip out of my role for one moment. But as I slowly travelled the road to my true role, Strong Ruk became my proper name.

In order for my journey west to be successful, I needed to spend as much time learning from Brother Peter in the monastery as I did from the oaks in the forest. I could be sitting beneath an oak one moment and in the monastery the next. But always I returned to my favourite giant oak, who was said to be hundreds of years old, for his wisdom was far greater than any man's could ever be.

Oaks taught me the advantage of using my wits, senses and courage; Brother Peter taught me the disadvantage of finding these qualities within myself. Oaks taught me the perils of retreating inside when problems arose; Brother Peter taught me to hide within myself the moment something began troubling me. And most

155

importantly, oaks taught me how to stand still when I needed to run; Brother Peter taught me how to run when I should have been standing still and facing my own fears.

Everything I began learning at the monastery was a stark contradiction to the education I was receiving from my people and from the ancient environment within which they lived. But only the education from my people offered me the opportunity to know the art of true reflection.

The more I saw of monastic life, the more certain I was that the monks were serving an apprenticeship under Beng's Locollico spirits. For while their daily prayers in the cloisters and their hearty singing in the choir and their care of the sick were impressive, they did very little to help the earth, sky, moon and sun. I never once heard any praise given to any of these ancient spirits of the Old Land; they were always left outside the big stony walls and the big stony souls of the men who lived behind them. To my mind, these men had failed their blood initiations; they were afraid to look life in the eye. Afraid of the political and religious power that was sweeping through communities everywhere, these unhappy men were willing to sacrifice their animal instincts and their relationship to the wild for the certainty of a place in heaven.

I have said that my people had no awareness of God. Well, we had no awareness of the Christian heaven either. Being familiar with the nature of roads, I told the monks that their road to heaven did not appeal to me and that it might just be a shadow road. But my argument became superfluous, for according to them, only one road, the road to God, could ever exist.

I learned to close my mouth when their eyes became glassy and their hands and faces turned pale. I could see the blood running from them whenever they were speaking their religious words in an attempt to convert me. I learned to play the heathen well, for they tolerated heathens and so long as I played their game they would treat me like an unusual pet. And so I escaped the punishment that other Christians might earn for themselves, because I was ignorant, just a fool. And their respect for Hawk, upon whose authority I was being schooled, probably had a hand in it as well.

My grandmother kept a watchful eye on me over the five years it took the monks to educate me. She made sure I never visited the monastery unless I was adorned with charms and urged me never to forget that every word spoken by religious men concealed venom and a double meaning and that every sword concealed a cross. The word and the sword had become dangerous in these times, she said. Neither were magical symbols any more. Just as she had become a rosebush, and just as men could become mountains and pastures and trees, so words and swords could become things that they were not.

She didn't have to press home her advice. I knew only too well how easily things could masquerade as other things. The experience in the ditch was something I would remember for the rest of my life.

And so I was able to remain strong within the confines of the monastery. And sometimes I would hear Peter saying in his soul, 'How wonderful it would be to be as happy as you are, Ruk, to be the hunter in the wood, to be the man who chases the girls, to be the man who is content to live with the sun, moon, earth and stars and to be as all men have been in the past: free.'

He never uttered any of these words of course, but I heard the intention clearly.

At other times, more worryingly, I saw his troubled eyes saying simply, 'Help me, Ruk. For I do not know where I am.'

In the five years that Peter was my teacher, there were many times when I knew he had been crying on his own. I often came upon him on his knees, praying for a sickness that would liberate him from the animal thoughts which troubled him during the night. And I prayed for his soul at those times, prayed that all our spirits would come to his aid, for I knew that Bitoso, the Locollico spirit who in his natural guise was a many-headed worm and who encouraged the monks to deprive themselves through fasting and denial, was drawing ever closer. It pained me to hear Peter say, after being at his prayers sometimes for an extraordinarily long time, that he felt better. For then I knew for certain that the squirming Bitoso was slowly eating his way into this poor man's soul.

What could I, a teenage heathen, do to help such a distinguished and literate young man who was in a far better position in society than I? I longed for him to learn to help himself. Over two years, I observed his happiness failing fast; in five years, the burden of unhappiness had woven deep into his soul and the spell already seemed irreversible.

Then I used to ask myself which one of us was living the real spiritual life and which one of us was the real pupil.

How I longed to take Peter home to my grand-mother. I would have asked our holy woman to help pull his soul back from the dark valleys of the creeping Lowerworld. I would have wanted him to find his own sword inside himself as a man and his own inner wisdom as a human being. And oh, I would have done so much for this man who became my friend, yes, so much, Chi.

I see him now, looking up at a tree, the oak that was just inside the monastery garden, his hand flattened against its trunk, as I had taught him, although he didn't know why he was doing it. I see him looking up into the branches and saying, 'Our world is really very beautiful, Ruk, isn't it?'

Rarely did he say such things, because beauty had at all times to be attributed to God and God alone; never would a tree have been permitted to exude its own beauty for its own sake and never would a tree have been permitted to become one's teacher.

But when Peter called the world ours, his words lingered with me. Rarely were Egyptians acknowledged as being in the same world as gaujos. And that told me that a little bit of Peter's soul was still intact and worth fight-ing for.

I look back and smile now when I think that Peter was supposed to be saving my soul when really, much of the time, I seemed to be saving his. There were so many occasions when our roles were in danger of reversing.

Peter didn't, of course, know anything about the task I was to carry out in England. He didn't even know of my plans to travel west. He only knew, from Hawk, that I needed educating in the proper manner. And he knew that Egyptians were nomadic, that they wandered about because they had no land and possessions of their own, largely, he supposed, because they were sinners. I saw no reason to explain my true purpose. And Uncle Hawk kept to his side of the bargain and rarely spoke a word about my forthcoming journey. Had Peter known the reason why he was schooling me, my guess is that he might never have offered his tutorship.

It wasn't easy. During those five years I can't remember the number of times I had to kneel and pray for forgiveness for 'sins' I hadn't committed. My knees were often stiff, even at my young age, and I grew tired of filling up my day with work that I didn't really need to do and that Christians seemed to revel in. I never understood the Christian principle that hard work and suffering make you good, because I never once saw anyone becoming good due to the suffering and hard work they had laid upon themselves.

According to the Egyptians, the gaujo world created its own sin. In fact it was a lie itself – the Boro Hukni, we called it. My grandmother said that religion gave the world a perfect opportunity to live out the greatest lie that had ever been. So whenever I was advised to renounce my heathen ways, I always ensured that I had a plentiful supply of salt on my person and my fingers tightly crossed, which meant I didn't have to mean any of what I was agreeing to at all.

But my frustration at all of this was soothed by the name that Peter gave me and that always made me proud: Thomas, he called me. My grandmother sneered at the name, but I liked it, because it made me feel that I was part of Peter's life, and I used it whenever I was with him and his brothers.

I was also uplifted by my regular visits to Hawk. In the largest room of the guest-house, much to the displeasure of some of the more fastidious monks, I received another important part of my education as he schooled me in the skills of the sword.

The monks did not like blood on their floors – or on their clean tablecloths. Blood, they maintained, could be spilled for God outside the monastery, but inside the only bloodletting should take place in the infirmary.

In many ways I understood why the brothers were so concerned. Many Locollico spirits were not only passive but also bloodless, and so neither blood nor aggression was permitted to flow in their presence.

At least Hawk was alive, even if he was an embodiment of aggression and sheer brutality. And no one could deny the passion with which he wielded a blade. He even impressed the monks with his adeptness.

It amused me once when Peter was invited to attend one of our mock battles. The monk sat on a stool watching us in his quiet attentive way.

'Ruk will be off to the holy land to become a true warrior before long, if he continues to exhibit such skills,' Hawk told him. This was a reference to my journey west. We had joked about it being a 'holy' pilgrimage somewhere. 'We shall have this heathen fighting for our true religion in the end.'

I saw Peter gulp as I grinned. Hawk handed me a sword, throwing back his head to laugh. He never seemed happier than when he was engaged in some kind of combat with others, either physical or verbal, and the monks were no exception to this.

Now he and I grinned at one other in that tense moment before friendly combat begins. And as I moved the heavy sword experimentally through the air, I saw what I could only describe as an envious look in Peter's eye. Then

I believed a memory was stirring in him, because I knew for sure that he had been a skilful swordsman before his commitment to monastic life. As he sat very still and somewhat stiff on the stool, I saw his deep longing to hold the sword and to wield it. And I imagined his own sword being eased from his hands and replaced by a cross.

At the end of my contest with Hawk, smiling and breathless in victory, I offered Peter the sword. As I stood there, and as Peter looked at the hilt being held under his nose, I felt his yearning for the forbidden and the intense passion welling up inside him. But then I felt the Lowerworld stirrings and the battle between his ancient soul and the creeping silence within him. I thought, I might have ended up like this myself had I permitted the Locollico to ease my own sword out of my arms.

Eventually Peter pushed the sword aside, smiling and saying, 'Thank you. No.' And he pushed his courage and passion back down inside himself – and left them there.

Yet I've no doubt that in the following hours he wrestled with his spirit and his conscience and went down on his knees. Perhaps he even cried. What did he really want from life? Did he ever know?

I am sure I must have been one of the most challenging pupils that he had ever known, because I know that there were so many times that I came close to converting him.

Eventually Hawk let me keep the sword I used in our mock battles. He said I had earned it. I had, after all, wounded him enough times with it – minor injuries he always laughed about and was proud to have.

I didn't tell him that whenever I used his sword I was also using my own magical sword. Hawk's sword projected itself upon my own and Uncle Iuzio's sword guided my hand into what Hawk described as 'some clever and complicated moves'. He often asked me where I had learned these skills and I told him that I honestly didn't know.

'You are a natural-born swordsman, a true warrior,'

he told me, sweating, bleeding, breathless and smiling.

He also told me that I could win myself some handsome prizes at the greatest tournaments: land, women, power.

But he knew I didn't want tournaments, or any wealth or prestige that they might bring. I only wanted to take my people home.

Over those five years my relationship with Uncle Hawk became almost congenial. And at last I discovered a softer side to him, although I still sometimes had to mind what I said in his presence.

As the fifth year approached I saw him becoming increasingly interested in the three monks I had cursed in the wood. I knew what he was looking for. He was waiting for them to show signs of splinters in their skin and dust on their habits. But as the fifth year dawned the three men had never looked healthier and this became a great source of anxiety for me, given that cursing was what I was supposed to be good at, perhaps even more than swordsmanship.

As that fifth year came to an end, I lay in my bed watching a merciless moon growing fat in the night sky through the door of my bender, wishing I could make some spell that would prevent time from moving on. I couldn't help visualising Hawk's anger as he realised that the curse had failed. I couldn't help feeling the sharp tip of his sword at my throat and I saw more than a little blood on the clean guest-house floor.

Finally, in desperation, I took myself to my grandmother.

'Has a curse ever gone wrong for you?' I asked. 'How many people have you cursed in your lifetime? How many curses succeeded and how many failed?'

She listened attentively and not without some amusement, squatting on her bender floor as my frantic questions rained down upon her like a shower of arrows.

'A great many of my curses came back at me, Ruk,' she confessed.

And that was all she said.

I walked out of her bender, in and out of it and up and down outside it for days. I desperately wanted to run away, but I knew it would be impossible. As Hawk had said, Div was an expert tracker, and his relationship with trees was beyond anything I had ever known. I envied his Keshali blood, but I hated the fact that his skills prevented me from going anywhere without him knowing about it.

All this time the three monks remained the same and even started to look smug about it.

Then, just a few days before the last moon became full, I was down at the river, praying to all our ancestors - yes, every single one – and hoping that someone somewhere could make things turn out right. Looking into the water, I saw Iuzio's reflection next to my own and I turned quickly to speak to him as he stood beside me on the bank.

'Iuzio, please tell me what to do. I am afraid. If these men are not cursed, I may not obtain my pass to take our people to England and my five years here with the monks will have been wasted and –'

He held up a reassuring hand.

'I know,' he said. 'Walk with me and we will talk about it.'

I followed him and we walked beside the river.

'Where is your sword, Ruk?'

'Here, uncle. Right here.'

'Have you been using it?'

'Yes, uncle. I have been using it when I've been with Hawk.'

He stopped and faced me.

'Only with Hawk?'

I didn't know how to answer this question.

'What did one of your grandmothers say to you about the sword, Ruk? What was the riddle she gave you?'

I blinked at him and rubbed my forehead, then remembered.

'What needs to be beloved and true and hateful and venomous all at the same time? And the answer is: a sword.'

'What do you think a curse is, Ruk?'

I thought about this, but confessed I didn't know the answer.

'And what do you think a blessing is?'

Again I looked at him blankly.

'A curse is a sword, Ruk. A blessing is a sword,' he said. 'And a blessing can be a curse while a curse can be a blessing. Think what happened when you were cursing those three monks.'

I did, and couldn't remember a thing.

'If you hadn't cursed them, Hawk would never have offered you the blessing of being able to go west. Your sword is not just for your hand, Ruk, it is also for your mind and your soul. Is the curse you laid hateful and venomous, or is it beloved and true? We cannot always see the greater value of what we do. We cannot always see the greater value of what others do either, sometimes until a much later time. Learn to think, Ruk. Learn to use your wits. Strength of spirit is also a warrior's way. Now come and look at what I have to show you.'

We walked close to the river's edge and I looked into the water.

Again, my image became clear and strong, and I held up the sword and saw that its image was also clear and strong. Then mists came and faces came. And there was one face there that I remembered seeing before, a young face in great confusion.

'Who is that?' I asked Iuzio.

'That is a child of yours, Ruk, a child of the future.'

'Where in the future?'

'Does it matter where in the future? Time plays tricks with us, Ruk. It doesn't matter where in the future your children are, just as it does not matter where in the past I am. Just remember to be as you are now and to pass on what you have now. That is all that matters.'

'My child seems so alone,' I said.

'Yes,' Iuzio said. 'Alone and afraid at times.'

'What can I do to help?'

Iuzio stepped closer to me.

'You lay a curse on three monks which a man overhears,' he said. 'The man then gives you a pass to go west so that you can take your people there. And once you are in the west there will be more opportunities to find our homeland and to help our child of the future meet our homeland. Need I say more?'

I looked up at him and saw the water's reflection washing over his kind face.

'You are the one who has the sword,' he said. 'You are the one who can provide the ending to this story.'

So, Chi, it was your face that helped me to return to my camp and to my grandmother and to face what I had to face.

I asked my grandmother to help me with the curse.

'I have been waiting for you to have the courage to come to talk to me about this, Ruk,' she said. 'And I have been waiting for you to talk to Iuzio, because I knew he would shout some sense into your ears. I lifted the curse a long time ago.'

'What!' I cried. 'Is that why the three monks aren't turning to dust? Or did you lift it because my curse had failed, because they wouldn't have turned to dust anyway and you wanted to spare me the embarrassment?'

My grandmother laughed as she sat beside her fire. Strings of herbs hung down from the ceiling, brushing our heads. There were many shadows because my grandmother liked to keep the bender darkened so that she could easily go into her trances. I always thought she looked especially ugly in the light of her fire. She had grown uglier as I had grown older. It was a holy woman's right to make herself ugly, she often told me. Evil spirits left the ugly alone.

She turned a pair of sad eyes upon me now. These were not ugly, but very beautiful – although she didn't like to hear me saying so.

'I know the three monks hurt you badly, Ruk, and I know they were very cruel to you, as many of them are to our people,' she said. 'I know they rightly deserved a curse and more. But I lifted the curse not only because you were unskilled in the art and should never have been meddling with such powers, but also for selfish reasons, my boy.'

She shuffled, a little embarrassed, then continued.

'I will have to live here with these monks after you have left us and gone west. Others who are older will have to stay here too. And you know how difficult that will be for us. But the monks may just provide for us and help us when there are hard times and when there is no one else here. Even if they are in their shadow worlds, we can work a little magic on them to help us when we are in need.'

She spat three times.

And I cut in. 'No. You will be coming west with us, grandmother. I have arranged for us all to go.'

She was shaking her head and laughing. 'No, Ruk. That is ridiculous. I would never be able to make such a journey. I would only hold you back. You know as well as I do that this cannot be. You do not need to do anything for me now. It is those who come after you who are going to need your help: your children, when you have them, and their children in the future. You know what Iuzio tells us about the Long Reflection, about passing our knowledge down. You will make a fine leader, a very fine chief and king, boy.'

Her hand was against the side of my face and I nestled against that familiar warm palm.

'How on earth can I ever do this without you?' I asked. 'I can't do this without you, grandmother.'

'Of course you can, my boy. And you will. I know, even though you are still only young, that you are already a warrior, which is your destiny, and that you will turn into a fine man. Our people will be proud of you and will always remember you. And you will always have Iuzio to guide you. He will continue to guide me too, here, in Little Egypt, and perhaps he will carry messages between us both. I just wish –'

She pulled her hand away, then gathered herself together in order to continue.

166

'I just wish I could be there to see you when you have finally grown into the man you will become. I wish I could see you in your new home.'

I took her hand and kissed her knuckles, holding her hand to my face again.

'But that is how it is to be,' she said, shrugging. 'None of us can stop the seasons moving. You must make this journey for all your people, Ruk, not just for me. It is time to do things for those in your future and for the little one we have both seen in the water.'

I was already weeping. 'But I don't know that child that we see,' I cried, wiping my eyes. I had plummeted into self-pity. 'That child is still just a stranger, grandmother. But you are dear to me now.'

She took my hand in hers, squeezing it tight.

'And you do not yet know your own children, but when you do you will be glad that you made this sacrifice for them. Don't you think that there was a time when Iuzio didn't know us? And look what he has always done for us – nothing has ever stopped him guiding and protecting us, has it? Nothing has stopped him pledging his life to us all and to the Long Reflection.'

She pulled me towards her. 'Don't cry, my boy,' she said. 'The child is still within you, but there again you are still young. You must learn to be strong, for me, for Iuzio, for Chi in the water and for us all. You must be strong for the Old Land and for what is to come.'

I was sobbing hard against her bosom, grabbing hold of the cloak she was wearing.

'But I'm frightened, grandmother,' I confessed. 'I'm so very frightened.'

I didn't know where these words came from, but they expressed how I was feeling deep in my soul.

'All warriors are frightened, Ruk,' she replied. 'Each and every one of us is afraid when we have a battle to fight, when we have to do something we've never done before. But you will have many of your people by your side on your journey west, and they will support you and help you along

167

the road. The young one we see in the water has no one, only us. That little one is very alone and very afraid. And our only hope is that this child will be able to remember us and preserve the life that could slip through our fingers if the Shadow World succeeds.'

She kissed my head. She rubbed my arms.

'Dry your eyes now, Ruk. Remember the lucky scars on your hands. And remember who you are. You know what our ancestors tell us about ancient memory.'

Yes. Remember, Chi, remember.

As I look upon your face now, reliving this memory with my grandmother and with all those in my past, I send the same message to you. I know that my grandmother was right. I know that what I did was right. And I did it for all my five children, but also for you. And I do everything I do for the Long Reflection and for the way life used to be. The ancient ways, the forgotten ways are so important to me, Chi. Our land here in the west is so important to me.

We always believe each journey must have an ending. We believe our road ends. But where does one journey end and another begin? Where are the joins? Remember how the road of life brings you and carries you away. Learning not the beginnings and endings but the nature of the journey itself will be the lesson that the road will provide you with, Chi.

This is something you will be called to think about in your life. And I hope you will think about it well. For we all move in circles and cycles, never in straight lines. We all desire to have another's path, another's easy life, but it is only ever our own life that can be lived and our own road that can be travelled. Remember this, Chi. Remember everything I am telling you.

I kiss my finger. My finger touches the water and your face.

I smile. I walk away from the river.

* * * * *

168

I collected the pass from Hawk. I also caught him standing reflecting beside one of the ponds on one or two occasions and I asked him to look more closely at his face, but he never really heard me and if he had he probably wouldn't have known what on earth I was talking about. I wondered what he had been thinking about while I had been talking to him. Perhaps his brother who was destined to be killed by my own hand? Had he any shame, any remorse? I didn't think so. I always saw Hawk as an entirely ruthless man and yet an intensely troubled one. And I was sure that he remained that way until the day he died.

When he gave me the pass, I was amazed. I had never seen anything like it before. It was written out on animal skin. Although we carved in wood, we did not have the skills to create powerful magical symbols with the feathers of birds. Some of us believed that writing would both change and curse the world.

When I walked away with that pass I was the proud possessor of a licence for me and my people to collect alms and to travel Europe for seven years as heathens doing penance. I had suggested that we should be allowed to travel for seven years as that was a magical number. My grandmother had said I should not travel unless this agreement was made and Div had suggested the same. Fortunately, Hawk had agreed to it. But little did he know that this pass would become a strong magical spell that would protect us wherever we went. We were able to wave it under people's noses and in a matter of minutes, or sometimes even seconds, procure food and shelter. But we could also threaten people with the strong authoritative magic imposed upon it by the powerful Hawk.

When I walked away from Hawk I had the feeling that I would never see him again, and I never did. My very last image of him remains with me. He is sitting quietly in the church, praying for strength, his hawk on his arm, a monk hovering nearby to sweep up the droppings from the tiled floor. It is perhaps the most thought-provoking image I ever had of the man.

When he had got to know me better, Div confessed to me that the only reason Hawk wanted to curse his brother was that he believed that he had at some time cursed him. When Div had been born, Hawk had thought that it was his brother who had caused a member of the Keshali to hop into his mistress's bed and to bring forth a child of the Otherworld. Once I arrived in England, his brother was destined to pay.

* * * * *

Finally the day came to leave. We had assembled our carts, wagons, horses and food, much of which had been provided by Hawk, and we were ready.

All the monks were sad to see me go. They were convinced I was ready for true conversion and perhaps even a life in the monastery. I know that they had been hoping that I would eventually join their order. But they were glad I was going on a great pilgrimage with my people to spread the word of God.

I still remember how difficult it was leaving Peter for the last time.

'You can come with us,' I told him eagerly, looking down from my horse as he stood blinking up at me in the sunlight. I wanted to tempt him. I was deliberately addressing his courage and passion.

'No,' he smiled, speaking in his usual quiet gentle fashion.

'What do you have to lose?' I asked him boldly.

'Nothing,' he confessed. 'Nothing at all. I just cannot come with you.'

'Why, uncle?'

He thought a while, then said, 'Because of who I am, Ruk.'

Because of who he was? I asked myself. Or because of who he had been before I came along?

How many times had I heard gaujos playing this game with themselves and each other, pitting the past against the future and using the past as a reason not to live for today?

How many times have I heard gaujos doing the same thing in the land I am living in now? People probably cling to their past just as much in your time, Chi.

But I also knew that Peter could not come with me because of the hold the Locollico spirits had on him. This hold, in my view, Chi, was far stronger than the hold of the Church.

Peter lifted his hand and touched my head. I can still see that pale hand offering me a blessing for the journey. 'A blessing or a curse?' I thought, as he spoke his Latin words and made the sign of the cross. I was hearing again the words of Iuzio, about how blessings become curses and curses become blessings.

I knew I wanted to leave Peter with my own blessing. I held his hand and squeezed it as he withdrew it.

'Godspeed, Ruk,' he said. 'May God go with you.'

And I thought I detected a tear in his eye as he produced a small wooden cross and gave it to me. It would protect me, he said. I thanked him and smiled. It might have been his own sword he was giving me, his own fight and passion hammered into its negative form by all those shadows he had wrestled with in the past. How I would have loved to have given him a real sword in return.

I turned my horse away and just as I reached the fringe of the wood I looked back and saw that he was still standing there. And we both stood looking at one another as if neither of us wanted to be the first to turn away. It was just as it had been when we had met on my first ever visit to the church.

Peter had been my friend for just five years of my life, but his influence would last me a lifetime. And just for one fleeting moment, perhaps one joyous moment, I believed that he might come running towards me, calling out for me to wait for him, begging me to take him with me. But he didn't. He simply stood there at the gate, watching me until I gave one final wave and turned my

171

horse along the woodland path, ducking my head under the low boughs. I knew that he would still be standing there watching me go, but I did not look back again.

But probably the worst thing I ever had to do was leave my grandmother. I had asked Peter to watch over her and had told him that if he didn't mind her spitting every time he mentioned God, she might just do something nice for him in return.

Now I stepped into my grandmother's bender for the last time. She was not alone. Many of the older ones were with her and even a few of the younger ones.

My grandmother looked up at me as I stood over her. 'You look like a man already,' she smiled.

'I'm not,' I said. 'Believe me, grandmother, I'm not.'

'Do you still have your sword?'

'Yes.'

'Hold it out for me.'

I unbuckled my sword, which was strapped to my back, and held it out to her. I believed she wouldn't be able to see it. But she closed her eyes and then I saw her running her bony fingers slowly, very slowly, across its blade and then along its hilt. It was the first time any other human being had held my sword, or even acknowledged that it was there. And when finally my grandmother took it into her hands, I was overjoyed.

She kept her eyes closed as she weighed it. 'It is extremely heavy,' she said. 'What needs to be beloved and true and hateful and venomous all at the same time?'

Surprised, I said, 'I didn't know you knew such a riddle.'

She smiled. 'You forget that I have known Iuzio a long time,' she said, 'far longer than you have. And I have also known many of our ancient grandmothers and grandfathers very well. Use this sword wisely, Ruk, as many of your ancient grandfathers have done.'

I buckled it onto my back again, then stood looking down at her.

'I don't want to go,' I said. 'I don't want to leave you, grandmother.'

I squatted down beside her. By this time she had opened her eyes. As she put her hand against my cheek for the last time, she said, 'Don't look back, Ruk. Never look back. Only look to your reflection. And there you'll always find me. Remember that you are going where I have always wanted to go. The west will be where our people will find their true home again, through that little one in the water. That must always be our hope. We cannot afford to think of anything else. The old world will come back to life in the west, one day. Keep remembering that. And ask yourself, are you really going that far? Will Iuzio be able to keep us all together?'

She laughed. And I laughed with her, but I was trying not to weep at the same time.

'Come now, Ruk. You are now a part of the great River of Life, a true image within the Long Reflection. You have been chosen to be a part of our Boro Dikimangro. That is a great honour.'

Then she whispered, *'Remember.'*

I kissed her hand fervently, then turned and walked out of the bender.

I know she followed me, as they all did. But when I mounted my horse and we started off, I didn't look back.

* * * * *

I left Little Egypt a boy, Chi, and I arrived in England a man. For seven years we wandered through towns and villages and settlements in western Europe, receiving alms wherever we went, thanks to Hawk's pass. I was honoured as a chieftain and the king of my tribe. I had become the youngest chief anyone in our tribe could ever remember and that was such a great honour for me.

King Thomas, my people had called me, in fun at first, just before we left Little Egypt. But the name stuck and I was honoured to be King Thomas, as well as Ruslo

Ruk, for the rest of my life.

Many of us took new 'Christian' names, but we still kept our Egyptian names, which we kept to ourselves. We made a vow to each other that we would never let our real names out into the bad magical gaujo world that was all around us.

My people soon learned that I had a secret sword given to me by one of our ancestors and they came to feel protected because of that, for I only had to touch the sword to gain strength and find answers when anyone asked me questions. So I used the sword for my wits as well as for my hand. Older men, including my father, and older women, including my mother, worked to help me lead my people in the right way. And I never made any decisions or did anything without our council's consent. Whenever I encountered a difficult problem I thought of my dear grandmother and wondered what her advice would have been. I saw her spitting many times when I made a mess of things, which I still did sometimes.

Wherever we went we spoke the Christian language, which was different from the language of our own people. We used gestures, signs and sometimes very few words to express ourselves. Christians and halfwits used words when they did not need to use them and I frequently heard them telling lies, as my grandmother had warned me. I learned English as well as French, and I spent a good many hours on my knees in churches and abbeys across the land, winning the favours of monks and sometimes even nuns.

My people learned to play their roles well, following my lead as a Christian pilgrim. But in the woodlands and behind the backs of the gaujos we would sit around our campfires laughing at that thing everyone called God.

And we discovered that we didn't always need to play our sacred game of Akahna, because we were given alms freely and most people were more than willing to help us. The game began to seem superfluous somehow. Things were changing very fast. Sometimes my people seemed to be losing their wits altogether.

Yes, Chi, seven years is a long time to spend on your knees and under the influence of the Locollico and the Lowerworld and under the shadow of the cross. The influence of the gaujo religion was sometimes so great that some of us were tempted to stray from our path, attracted by the many pleasures and securities that the gaujo religion can bring.

I saw a sleep overcoming many of our people, Chi; I saw them stretching and yawning and making their beds ready, beds that were really tombs in disguise. And I saw shadows standing by, ready to creep up and ease their souls away, just as mine had very nearly been eased away in my Jal Raht initiation in the ditch.

When we left Little Egypt we were a group of around eighty and on landing on English soil we were just twenty-five. Yes, Chi, that is how badly the gaujo religion affects people and takes their wild spirits away. In just seven years our numbers and our spirits had dwindled, because the shadows in the world had become so strong.

But those who stayed with me remained loyal to what we knew to be true. We kept our knowledge sacred and the Long Reflection in our hearts. We had to keep strong. For the further we went, the more the social climate changed. The churches and the Christian faith were losing their earlier flexibility and finally beginning to turn to stone and dust. We saw this happening before our eyes.

I saw that there was no longer a look of regret in the faces of the pious, a look of having left something behind, as I had seen in Brother Peter and his brothers. People now believed, wholeheartedly, that living with fear and worry and grief was normal, because their parents had lived in this way and their grandparents had lived in this way. And I saw their own Long Reflection stretching away from them into future generations, containing only images of shadow and dust where real life used to be.

I feared for them, Chi, and for the future of us all. Meanwhile, they were fearing for me, for the simple heathen who still had so much to learn. I read the message in their eyes over and over again: 'He knows nothing. This heathen is to be pitied.'

Most of all I feared for all those who had been encouraged to forget.

* * * * *

Now that I am at the end of my journey rather than at the beginning, I must let you decide for yourself how to judge my last ever visit to a monastery. I hope you will think about this with your soul, Chi. For it is something I would like to leave you with.

Yes, I want to return you to that last visit, to the time when I could not get up off the floor because of being weighed down by all the spoils concealed in the lining of my robe.

There is more to tell you here.

You see, Chi, when you enter the churches now it is evident that a great curse has been laid. I know that this will be very much the same in your time. See the coloured sunlight streaming through the stained-glass windows. See the silver and the gold and the power. And remember that this was stolen from the magical Otherworld a long, long time ago.

Now the colour from the windows and the gold and the silver are no longer sacred, for they have taken on the spirit of the Shadow World. The whispering that can be heard within the thick walls will be loud when you stand in the quietness of the aisles, for the shadows in these places will be speaking to you directly.

Now the shadows have been able to find a home and the great hood worn by the spirit I met in the ditch has been pulled across the heads of all those who enter the dwelling. Gently, meekly, silently it falls, so as not to be noticed, as the spirit of Bitoso eases the swords out of the hands of those who would be courageous and strong, diluting the passion that is within them, luring them into a permanent sleep. A sleep, yes, Chi, a sleep within the darkness that creeps slowly across the land, like a cloud that is bringing rain or snow, except this is not rain or snow, this is sorrow and guilt and grief and pain. Many people will fall into this deep slumber and just not know who they are or where they are any more.

You may have felt this way yourself, Chi. And you may also feel that this is coming to you.

But I am here to give you hope.

I know now that the spirit who took my sword from me in the ditch was Bitoso, the many-headed worm who is all about disease. I have seen the effects of disease, the plague that has raged around us, sent by God, they say – but more truthfully by Beng in his Shadow World.

Do you think that your ancient grandfather was stealing all the riches from the churches, Chi? Or do you believe that he was doing what our people have always done: showing others that we cannot continue drinking from fountains just because the water is there? Because that is what people are doing today. That is how they are creating their disease. When is gold not gold, Chi? You know this riddle, don't you? You have already heard it from one of your most beloved and beautiful grandmothers. When is a sword not a sword? And what falls down and gets up again for the good or for the bad?

I know. You will say, 'Please, no more riddles, grandfather.'

The journey of life will be within you to complete, Chi, just as it has been within me. Remember that the journey matters. Remember what I have said about roads. Remember the words of your ancient grandfather and the words of all your grandfathers and grandmothers who came before you. And remember Iuzio, our most beloved ancestor. He will affect you in unusual ways. When you think he is doing you no good at all, that is usually when he will be doing you the most good, and teaching you the most too.

I am now about to become a grandfather and about

177

to start off on another road: the road to being a grandparent. And I wonder how many generations will pass before you are here walking the earth yourself. Perhaps you will stand where I am standing now, upon this very spot overlooking the near water tossing its beautiful dancing stars into the air.

We have settled here in the Weald because it is so untouched. The woodlands hum with the old magic and our ancestors' voices are loud here.

Sometimes I still think of my grandmother, that wonderful woman I was forced to leave so long ago. Iuzio kept me in touch with her during my seven-year journey west. When I asked him if she was happy, he said she was, knowing I had taken our people west at last.

We had been journeying west for so long, you see, Chi, from our homeland in the east, and for far too long bandits and warring tribes had tormented us, chasing us wherever we went and trying to cut us down. So when we found a little peace in Little Egypt, we stayed a long time. And some of us stopped travelling with the sun. My grandmother and many other elders were troubled by this. But not purely because we had stopped travelling.

'We will never reunite with our homeland in the Otherworld if we do not continue moving along the path of the sun,' my grandmother used to say. 'The sun moves from east to west and we must do the same, especially inside ourselves. The sun knows his Otherworld home because he never stops moving through the seasons.'

She explained that we did not simply travel through the seasons on the earth, we travelled through the seasons in our inner landscape as well. If you travelled across the earth without travelling across your inner landscape, you would never really be travelling at all. And all the time we were journeying west I kept this valuable knowledge in mind, seeing many dawns and many sunsets, and asking the sun always to guide us home.

I remembered only too well Iuzio's words: 'What is a road, Ruk? Do you know what a road is?' What moves without moving? A road is less about distance, more about discovery. I come from the place you have not yet found, Ruk, but it is also the place you never really left behind.'

I also remembered those valuable words spoken by one of my ancient grandmothers: 'Ask yourself, Ruk, are you within Little Egypt or is Little Egypt within you? Is Ruk within England or is England within Ruk?'

And now I tell myself: 'England, the landscape, is within me. For although I have travelled west, I have travelled a road to the sun in my soul. I have come to understand the nature of roads very well. And the nature of swords. And also the nature of oaks, which are plentiful here in the Weald.'

One day I heard from Iuzio that my grandmother had died. 'You must let her go now, Ruk,' he said. 'Puv, the earth, will now look after her flesh, and Ravnos, the air, will now look after her breath. Kam, the sun, will look after her blood, and Shon, the moon, will look after her water. She is safe. But you must release her spirit to these places now and permit her to step into her new life.'

When I heard this, I cried hard on my knees, deep in the forest alone. I was sorry that I had not been there to ease her passing. But I knew that Iuzio was right, for we must allow those we love to return to the Greater Ancestors who are our creators. To hold on to them is to create a shackle in the hereafter, within the Otherworld.

I know you will be wondering whether I laid the curse when I finally arrived in England and whether I killed Hawk's brother.

Well, I didn't need to carry out the curse at all. For when I arrived in England I discovered that the man I was supposed to be hunting down was already stricken with a curse that had been laid by some other hand in some other way. He was already living under the shadow of the cross in a monastery infirmary. By the time we reached our destination he was already a dying man.

I knew that it would be enough for Hawk to discover that his brother was ill. It would be enough to know that he was now doing penance for his sins. Whether he would believe that I myself had laid the curse didn't matter. But we never got to tell Uncle Hawk this news, for we heard that he had died in battle somewhere far away, although another rumour went about that he had died in a drunken brawl. I didn't know which to believe. And perhaps it didn't matter, because he was honoured as a hero on his estate, his Egyptian mistress mourned him and Div continued to idolise him. He always tells people about his two fathers: the father who was a member of the Keshali race, from another world, and the father who was a knight and who died in battle and became a hero. Div has remained with our tribe and continues to be my trusted friend and adviser.

Would I have killed Hawk's brother, had circumstances been different?

I must leave that for you to decide, Chi. I must leave you to reflect on Iuzio's words about fate and about the roles different people play in our lives.

* * * * *

And so we made it west after all. We followed the path of the sun, the road that curls up within the smoke away into the sky. And I did not become distracted by any veiled women. I found myself a very beautiful wife who also understood roads and she has taught me a good deal in the time I have been with her. We have five beautiful children and now there will be grandchildren as well. And I know that one of those, Chi, will play their part in the story of the Long Reflection and continue the journey.

We have integrated into the woodland here very well. We are respected by many of the people who live around us and we do our best to help them where we can. I converse sometimes with the woodland folk and Div has helped me to understand their intricate and magical ways far more than ever before. I have taught my children to count the drops of water strung along the branches whenever it has rained, in memory of my dear grandmother. And I hope they will pass this knowledge on to their own children when that time comes, so that the woodland folk remain happy and continue to trust us.

But *remember* now, Chi. Yes, when you see my face I want you to remember, as my grandmother and Iuzio advised us to do.

We came beyond the water, which was once so far away, didn't we? And I carried out a task which I thought impossible, didn't I? We did it. We did all of it.

And I know that you will go beyond the water too, in your soul. You'll go beyond your reflection within the River of Life. You must remember to stand very tall and very proud wherever you go and whatever you do, just as one of your ancient grandfathers did. You must remember that fear is all part of understanding what courage is about.

Keep strong, Chi, when troubled times come your way. These strong arms, and more importantly this strong heart, will still be here whenever you look in the water.

And if you really look, Chi, sometimes you may just see my sword dancing before your eyes.

The Age of Hala

Iuzio the Immortal's Second Tale

'So, look. Will you take the time now to look?'

'Why should I look?' you might ask.

'Because if you never look at yourself how will you ever know that you are there?'

'Don't be absurd,' you will argue. 'Of course I am *there*, because when I look at my reflection I can only ever see myself, can't I?'

'Can you?' I ask. 'Can you really?'

* * * * *

I pace up and down, up and down, in a cave in the Homelands, thinking of you, Chi. I think of Horki and Ruk, and all of you.

Sometimes I pace for so long that I forget where I am and I have to stop to look at my reflection in a small rockpool at the mouth of the cave. And it is then that I think: This task is so hard. Perhaps it is too hard.

But I need to keep strong. Always I have to be strong.

Such is the life I live, Chi, one foot in the mortal world and the other in the immortal world, always concerned for those who are in danger of falling into the Shadow Lands, as Horki and Ruk almost did, and as others who are to follow will almost certainly do. And what they all do will affect you, Chi. You know that by now, don't you? And perhaps you also now know that you will be the most endangered of all, because of the growing strength of the curse upon our world.

I don't think anyone really knows how hard it is for me here alone, trying to work a magic that has been crushed, just as the ancient world has been crushed, because in reality no true immortal was ever meant to live in the mortal world in the way I do. The World of Mortals was very different in earlier times.

And you know that because of the task I have chosen to perform I am bound to a mortal way of life, whatever it chooses to bring me. Yes, Chi, I am unavoidably thrust into the World of Time every time I take but a step into the changed mortal world. And you probably already know that within the World of Time we are in danger of forgetting our Ancestral Homelands.

It feels strangely comforting to tell you all of this, Chi. For there are few mortals I can talk to, so busy are they coping with the daily problems associated with mortality. Mortals rarely accept that they are mortal, you see, Chi. That is usually their biggest and only problem. Mortals are looking for the unreachable: the sun that never rises.

Yes, Chi, just as immortals can play at being mortal, so a mortal can play at being immortal, and if they don't get it right, and don't understand what they are doing, they may be guilty of weaving uncertainty and doubt into the Great Fabric of Life, which will open the door to shadow.

For should you as a mortal ever be tempted to step into what we immortals refer to as the Eternal Mortal Self, oh Chi, you will find yourself stepping into a very dark and dangerous place, far more dangerous than Horki's cave or Golden City, and far more dangerous than Ruk's ditch. You will be inviting shadows to dance as you become their eternal puppet.

Can you relate to what I am saying here, Chi? Can you relate to your desire to be eternal?

And you may say to me, 'But where were you then, Iuzio, when Horki and Ruk were going through their terrible ordeals? Why didn't you step in to help them?'

Yes, I can hear you asking such questions.

And I would say, 'Why doesn't a mouse help an elephant to scurry? Why doesn't a fish teach a bird to breathe underwater?' Because, Chi, we have no right to stop others doing what they need to do for themselves. My helping Horki out of Ana's tent and helping Ruk out of his dark ditch would have been as pointless and as inappropriate as a mouse teaching an elephant to scurry. We immortals must stand back and allow lessons to be learned at the time that they need to be learned.

And of immortality you may say, 'Of course I don't think I am going to live forever, Iuzio. I want to learn the lessons I need to learn. Of course I believe that one day I am going to die. I *accept* that I am mortal.'

Do you? So why do you hang on to so much inside yourself then, when you could let it all go? Why do you keep people and things locked away in a part of yourself where you are able to keep them all under your control – and keep them that way forever? You claim to be mortal, but how often do you exhibit mortal ways? You constantly play at being immortal.

At the very worst you could become trapped within the World of Time, especially if you refuse to learn the valuable lessons which mortality teaches you. You need to earn the right to become mortal before you can ever earn the right to become immortal. True immortality is but a small spark within you at this moment, waiting for the chance to dream.

But so is mortality.

And you will probably have wondered who I am exactly. Who is this person, this being who walks into people's lives and follows them everywhere they go?

I hope you'll understand that I am that immortal spark in an ancient line of Egyptians, a line so old that it affects many mortals who are still in the Indo-European world today. I am the seed of earlier life, an integral part of the natural world, just as sunlight is an integral part of summer and snow is an integral part of winter.

And although this may be hard for you to understand, my hope is that together we will find the key that will reverse the curse and rebuild the bridge connecting the mortal and immortal worlds.

Oh, there is much to tell you about the curse, Chi, so very much.

If you and I are able to reflect once more upon Horki's challenges, and upon Ruk's challenges, and upon the challenges you find within your own life, and if you can understand how these shape your life, we can begin to see more clearly what is going on.

I would not rest, you see, Chi, if I didn't do something about this situation. I would be pacing up and down here in my ancestral cave in our beautiful Homelands forever. And what good would that do any of us?

For there was never an age when the chasm between our two worlds stretched so wide. That chasm has now become immeasurable. It deepens with every passing moment. It is deepening now as I speak. It is a dark hole of such unimaginable proportions, an abyss so deep that it appears to be bottomless. You might call it hell. And it is in danger of claiming you, should you take but one small step towards it, as Horki did, and as Ruk did. We immortals call it the Boro Kaulo Hev – the Great Black Hole.

This hole was always there. But many thousands of years ago it was far shallower and not half as wide. And time was different then, too, Chi. So many things were different. And that is because awareness of power was different. But power was soon used to control the World of Time. And now you only have to look around you to see how the World of Time controls you.

Yes, you know it is serious, don't you, Chi?

And the River of Life has long been affected by the perils of Hala.

Learn this word, Chi, for it is a word you will hear me using often in the future; it is the one great enemy of both mortal and immortal worlds.

You might say that Hala is the corruption of time and power. We immortals call the age you are living in 'the Age of Hala'. To mortals it will seem to have lasted for thousands of years. To immortals it is but a season, albeit a prolonged one, like a stubborn cold winter that is taking its time to pass.

But Hala in the ancient language of immortals means 'the Time of the Curse', and it also means 'the Number of the Curse'. And it can mean 'Shadow walks with you'.

Hala in the language of mortals, or the Blind World, or the world in which you live, means 'an expanse of Time through which the Curse will be done'.

Hala also means 'century', Chi.

Does that surprise you? Perhaps you will say, 'Ah, now I understand.'

You will learn about the Eleventh Hala, which Horki walked through, and the Thirteenth Hala, which Ruk walked through, and the Fifteenth Hala, which you will see Lenore and Lileskai walking through, and the Seventeenth Hala, which you will see No Name walking through. All their stories are important for you to learn, Chi.

And ask yourself this: Are centuries needed to make the seasons work? Is the World of Time necessary in the construction of our lives? Do centuries build dwellings and roads? Or do the dwellings and roads build centuries?

Perhaps this seems nonsensical to you, but think about it, Chi.

Does Time build anything at all? Does everything take Time? Or does Time take everything? Might it be that Time has been stretched across the world like a great blanket, suffocating mortals, blinding them to their true tasks in life?

186

Centuries of Time become Hala as soon as they have a bearing on what you do.

So never forget what a century means, Chi. When Ruk was told by the monks 'in the year of our Lord', he was also being reminded that he was in Hala, rather than a seasonal cycle.

You see, you cannot have Hala unless you have Time and you cannot have Time unless you have Hala. And you cannot have Hala unless you have Power and you cannot have Power unless you have Hala. These are a close family of shadows who live together and spend their time plotting and scheming and wreaking havoc upon the world. Remember 'the expanse of Time through which the Curse will be done'. Understand this and you will understand that time and Time are very different, Chi. And you will not allow yourself to be enchanted by Hala.

You may have many questions about this word. I hope you will have many questions about this word. For you may already have noticed that few people ask questions when answers appear to bring more knowledge.

'To know all' is one of the many traps of the Great Curse, as are 'to be all' and 'to have all'. It is the *all* that holds the power. For if mortals do not have *all*, they are worried that they will fall down and become nothing.

And I want to tell you now that those in the Shadow Lands spend a lot of their time doing nothing. They sit around yawning. And they watch and wait as an individual's time of Jal Raht approaches, which, as you know, is the puberty years. And as each mortal child grows into adulthood, the shadows gather together, because, after all, it gives them something to do. And wherever they detect weakness, they put on the pressure. They know who is likely to become a halfwit. They also know who is likely to exhibit the courage of Ruk in the dark ditch and the common sense of Horki in Ana's tent, in which case they will think twice and leave such young ones alone.

And the shadows stand by with their shadow cloaks which they cannot wait to throw around an individual's

187

shoulders, Chi. And should an individual fail to realise that she is in Ana's tent and being deceived, or that he is lying in a ditch and being deceived, the shadows will not depart. No, they will *never* depart, but will remain at that person's side forever, pretending to be their humble servants. And their cloaks will have been wrapped tightly around them, supposedly to keep them snug and warm and safe. But whoever heard of a cloak of nothingness keeping anyone snug and warm and safe?

It is laughable, Chi, isn't it? I hope you are laughing. Even though this is a serious matter, it will be good if I hear you chuckling to yourself.

Let me tell you that there are many shadow cloaks, all fashioned, knotted and woven lovingly by many pairs of bloodless hands. This might bring a chill to your spine if you do not find it ridiculous. Because in reality there is only One cloak that can ever be fashioned in this way. For there can only ever be One such Pattern, One such Design. And all the bloodless hands are busily at work in the One Way and at the One Time, all the nimble fingers moving together to create a garment of nothingness, fashioned to last forever. All the workers are willing, all performing the task out of love. But all are being deceived about the true nature of the garment.

And if you look closely enough you will see how uneven the weave is. It is messy, untidy, and no skill has been deployed. A true craftsman would throw back his head and laugh at such handiwork.

Would you recognise this untidiness, this weave, this cloak, if you saw it, Chi?

You would first have to recognise the halfwit within yourself.

Yes, looking upon yourself as a halfwit would shake you. For already halfwits have earned themselves an unfavourable reputation in our stories.

But know that a halfwit will earn the right to own the Great Cloak of Arrogance without too much trouble. And this is probably the strongest cloak of all.

And it may surprise you to learn that shadow cloaks can only be worn beneath the fleshy exterior – yes, like wearing clothes on the inside. It is an inside-out process, Chi.

Does this surprise you? Perhaps it won't by now.

Eventually, if too much time passes by, the very soul of a person may become woven into the fabric of the cloak. Yes, Chi, it is all laughable up until this time, but then it isn't funny any more. For as soon as you have been woven into a shadow's dusty fabric, your soul has gone.

And you might ask, 'Is it really possible to wear clothes on the inside, Iuzio? For if that is so, who would be able to see what I was wearing?'

The answer will lie concealed in your question, Chi.

Say the question again, hear the question again and see if you can't find the answer.

I call these cloaks 'shadow play'. You may refer to them as 'avoidance', 'pushing things under the carpet' or 'assuming airs and graces'. The cloak called Flesh has become a mask today, Chi, a shield, something to hide behind. It is no longer a vehicle for the soul's expression.

You must set about relinquishing your loyalty to shadows, Chi, by relinquishing the gifts they constantly lay at your feet. You will need to know the difference between a gift and a shackle. And when you do, you will receive an invitation from all those in the Realms of Souls. The Realms of Souls, where the real people are, will be reaching out their hands to help you, inviting you to join them. And then you will be safe.

But for now, remember to keep asking those questions, Chi, and looking for answers within the questions.

And I again remind you to *remember*.

* * * * *

So, I, Iuzio the Immortal, began the original journey within the River of Life. But this journey did not start in time. No. It started in the World of Time.

189

I will explain what I mean.

The journey began when the skies began to darken, which they had never done before, and when the landscape began to froth and foam and spout fire and turn itself upside down and inside out, which it had never done before.

This brought an end to what we long referred to as the Golden Age. And Hala was created. And my image had to be cast into the river quickly, so that it went unnoticed by those who might have caused more harm. And over thousands of years my image sealed itself within ice floes, and within some of the greatest mountain ranges and valleys, and within some of the great rocks of the world. Yes, the River of Life flowed deep into ages that are beyond human memory now, Chi.

And Pahni, the spirit of water, protected my immortal reflection. While your soul was sleeping within the mists of time, this beautiful spirit was capturing and recording faces, passing them between the tides and along many channels in the hope that they might replace the bad images that might do mortals harm.

Faces that were good and faces that were bad – who at that time, as now, could tell one from the other? They were grinning and grotesque, or smiling and sweet, here a contorted grimace, there a vain scowl, and somewhere Horki's slobbering old man. And all of them being washed up on the shores of the world.

Yes, it is still very much the same today. For when you paddle in a river or the sea, or lie on a beach with water lapping over you, can you ever be sure who – or, more appropriately, what – might be washing over you from the past?

The world, Chi, is still full of so many strange images.

So you must also be careful what you are thinking when you are in the presence of water; you must be careful what you wish for. Because it is all too easy to wish a dark spell upon yourself.

You probably didn't know that all mortals' wishes

come true when they are uttered in the presence of water, did you?

'How can that be, Iuzio?' you might ask. 'I have wished for so many things so many times in the presence of water and still I am waiting for these things to materialise.'

Haven't they materialised? Look again. Haven't you been the recipient of things you say you didn't ask for? Haven't you heard people saying 'I never asked for this'?

That is the kind of dark spell I am talking about, Chi: all your wishes will come true, but never in the way you expect them to.

And wishes will never help you while you are choosing shadows as partners and shadows as guides and while you are choosing not to manage your affairs in the way a natural mortal should.

The shadows made it plain to Horki and Ruk that wishing for beauty and warriorship would transport them to an ideal world, but a world which would make them bend to the whims of yet more shadows.

Only when one sees clearly what is going on will one see the illusions that are taking place.

So, should you say to yourself, 'I wish I were rich' or 'I wish I were poor', I assure you that such a wish *will* come to pass, but probably not in the way you expect it to. Shadows will cause us to wish for illusions, yet in our hearts we will be certain that such wishes are good and true, because we believe they are what we need to make our lives complete.

And this is because mortals make wishes with immortal intentions. Should a mortal's wish come true in an immortal way, the results of that wish may just be destined to last for an eternity.

And what will you do then with something you swear you never asked for?

And though you may have forgotten what you saw of yourself when you looked at your face in the river, maybe only yesterday, it is true that the water will never forget what she has seen of you. For she is fated always to remember. And she remembers the games you have played with immortality and she will simply leave you to your fate.

It is wise to remember that Pahni has a memory far stronger than the memory of any immortal spirit, far stronger than the spirit of fire, who remembers the sun, far stronger than the spirit of air, who remembers the sky, far stronger than the spirit of earth, who remembers the mountains and woodlands and the great forests of the world. Our Lady of the Water is destined to remember everything that has ever flowed through her rivers, oceans and streams. So, in just a small trickle, you may discover a long, long memory of faces and wishes past.

And sadly, in many places across the earth, Pahni has been forced to reduce herself to the smallest trickle.

And even though my own immortal image continues to flow within her waves and ripples, people do not see my image as they might have done long ago.

You see, before the Age of Hala, water flowed into and out of people's mouths, eyes and ears as well as in and out of the rivers. And Pahni was willing to honour them with her great secrets in exchange for their loyalty to the water within themselves, to their own emotions.

Know, Chi, that because Pahni's intentions have been abused, she rarely visits the World of Mortals now and chooses instead to live out her days alone in the Ancestral Homelands. Her refuge is within a collection of mysterious caves in the depths of the immortal world, a place no mortal will ever be able to find, for it is beyond mortals' capacity to see.

But within these Homelands the old ones, the spirits of water, fire, air and earth, can safely reside, away from all those who would abuse them. And as long as shadows are invited to dance in mortals' eyes, and as long as lessons are devalued, and blood initiations sacrificed, and vows to mature broken, they will remain there, longing, always longing for news of a return to the old ways. They rush to their doors sometimes when an immortal like me returns to them. 'What news? What news?' they will cry. And we hang our heads. For there is no news that will give them what they are looking for: an opportunity to engage with the World of Mortals as they once did. They must sit things out until the Great Curse is done; they must wait until all those generations who follow Horki have played their part.

They must also wait for you, Chi.

And many times I have heard Pahni say that she will continue to abstain from assisting mortals as long as their thirst for immortal power prevails. She is strict, but she is also wise. Know that she would once easily have been your friend and guide, Chi, just as I am; yes, she would have done a good deal to help you in another era.

Know that as the One's Great Curse took hold, in the beginnings of Hala, many thousands of years ago, there fell a great and deepening silence over all the earth where water had once flowed. And this was a drought of the soul, an emptiness that both parched and chilled the human spirit.

Oh, there was a time when all you had to do was listen and you could hear the water whispering and laughing in your ears. There was a time when Perri the Mortal, who lived a long time before Horki and Ruk, was able to hear Pahni singing him the old songs on warm summer evenings and laughing as her ice broke on cold winter mornings. And her spirit filled him with such a great happiness. But soon the absence of music from water was bringing a silence to his life and a silence to the whole earth.

And still this silence prevails today.

It is not good news, Chi, for the soul's great drought has grown from childhood into youth and he is now a restless and mischievous young man. And nobody would believe how it all once used to be, in our Golden Age long ago.

Now we may believe that we are seeing beautiful Pahni and her water when she flows across the earth. But we may just be looking at dust.

Yes, Chi, as hard as this is to believe, it is true.

193

What mortal would believe that water could turn to dust? But all things, both animate and inanimate, may just turn to dust if the spirit of water chooses to depart from them, for all things need to contain Pahni's spirit in order to remain alive.

There was once no place on earth where water did not flow. Now there is hardly a place where water does flow.

An absence of water disturbs and weakens the spirit, enabling a shadow to take on its elemental form and to begin building its home, usually before anyone has had time to notice what is going on.

The Shadow Lands are worlds of cloaks and masks and hoods, Chi, which you already know. They are places born of the hidden and the unspoken, realms given life by all that is obscure, which you already know. But know also now that the Realms of Souls are worlds of flesh, presence, passion, laughter and all that is unambiguous and true. And these worlds will be open to you should you choose to see yourself as you are.

And then there is the Bald Landscape, hidden far away in the wilderness of the Shadow Lands. I have to mention this, because it has become a popular place. But in reality it is the most desolate and inhospitable place anywhere: devoid of life, death, pain, joy, fear and feeling. Yes, devoid of all water, a vast wasteland across which you are actually unable to travel, because there is nowhere you can go, and you are therefore fated never to reach your destination.

Yes, Chi, can you imagine moving but not moving at all? Perhaps you can. Perhaps you recall visiting this place once in a dream.

I said it was popular, and that is because many are enticed to visit it in their dreams.

But know that upon the Bald Landscape you will find only the driest dust, a fine powdery grey film of it, freshly carpeting the ground. And yet there is no ground. For should you kneel down and dig your fingers deep into the soil upon this great plain you will discover that there is no soil, for it will crumble to nothing as soon as you make contact with it. Yes, you will actually see it disappearing before your eyes. In fact, if you rub such dust between your finger and thumb, you will realise how very old and elusive it is, older than Horki's time, older than Perri's time, older than any mortal's time, and more elusive than the most elusive of dreams. So you will not be able to hold this dust for very long, Chi, because all too soon it will have disappeared.

Hope is a lost memory in this place.

And when you look up at the night sky from the Bald Landscape you will see no stars, just as in the day you will see no sun. For this place contains no heaven upon which stars may rest and no sky upon which a sun may burn. You will see no rainbows, no dawns or sunsets. You can light no fire to warm yourself, for there is no solid ground upon which fire may burn, and you cannot dig up any water to drink, for there are no channels through which water may flow.

The only object you are likely to see upon the journey you are desperately trying to make is a great dwelling on the far horizon. Is there a horizon? By this time you will be asking such a question. And yet you will be certain that there is something there on the edge of the land, looming and shimmering like a mirage in a hazy mist; you just won't know whether it is real or unreal. But when you see it, it may look so comforting that you won't care, because you will be glad to see anything at all in this cold empty place.

This dwelling, you will observe, is a huge castle rising up and adorning the great skyline. It is tall, wide, turreted and magnificent, with banners flying on a gentle wind that does not blow and walls gleaming in sunshine that gives no light. You will see it hanging on the edge of an abandoned eternity in this vast Bengesko realm. It will be inviting as it winks at you in the eerie light like a precious jewel shining out of a cold empty casket.

And you will probably have heard by this time that

195

Beng dwells there.

And if there is any of your soul left in you at all, you will realise that this castle was the first ever castle to be built and is therefore considered to be the greatest fortress of all. But it is a dwelling that can only ever bask in the silent distance; it will never draw near and it will never recede. You will be destined never to reach it, just as you will be destined never to move away from it. For such is the dark magic of the Bald Landscape, such is the dark spell of cloak and mask and hood, deception, ambiguity, uncertainty and doubt, which is all you will ever find in the great wilderness of the Bengesko realms.

Mortals who look for water, Chi, mortals who attempt to understand how water moves and flows and breathes, moving as much in the depths as in the shallows, flowing as much in the trickling streams as in the great waves, breathing as much in tiny ripples as in the rhythm of the great tides, will not be banished to these realms in the Shadow Lands. Mortals who know water will be offered solace, a place of safety, in the Realms of Souls.

Go and find some water now, Chi, and let us make contact with it. Allow it to run through your fingers slowly. And then let it run across your skin and onto your body, and into your mouth, and onto your tongue, and down your throat, and deep into your belly. Think then about water and what it is. And allow yourself to speak with the voice of water, with the voice of a river.

And if you should find yourself speaking with the voice of dust – which means you will not be able to say much at all – you will know that your spirit may well be departing and in fact may already have gone. And you will know that this is a sign that you have been visiting the Bald Landscape and we will need to bring your spirit back home again.

Do not despair if this is how life feels. For there is hope now that I am here beside you.

Just don't fool yourself, Chi. Now is the time for what is real.

I know it will surprise you if you suddenly hear yourself speaking with the voice of dust, because you will not have been aware of speaking in this way before. You will find that as soon as you feel you want to say something, you will rather not say it, because dust will quickly clog up your mouth, your throat, your eyes, your ears and every orifice. And you will feel fear in many regions of your body, as those parts become congested: all these little tight bundles of dust gathering together across your body, created by shadow and attracting yet more shadow.

And you will think: Dust doesn't make waves or rock my boat. That which does not move or flow cannot harm me, surely. It is better that I am still.

But are you still or have you become static? Are you calm or are you unable to move?

Look at the dust beneath your feet, Chi. Do you ever see it moving? It will only move by the hand of the spirit of the wind, by the power of some external force. It has no life of its own.

Dust can never flow; it can only ever spread. Dust can never breathe; it can only ever shift. Dust can never wash; it can only ever suffocate and blind. Dust will sing you no songs, as water will.

Understand that dust is dead, Chi.

Should you go and find some dust, with the intention of letting it run through your fingers and across your skin, and onto your body, and into your mouth, and down your throat, and deep into your belly, just as you did with water, well ... need I say more?

Did you ever see water casting a shadow? Look now for the shadows cast by water. And let me know when you have found them. For I will come and look at them with you if you will show me where they are.

Water can only ever cast reflections, Chi. Water is incapable of casting shadows. And that is because she feels.

And you will say, 'Iuzio, I believe I am beginning to *feel* again.'

And that will please Pahni, who is waiting for your mortal story to unfold.

Do you know the Mortal's Story, Chi?

There once was a man who lived and died,
lived and died, lived and died.
To become a mortal he died and lived,
died and lived, died and lived.
To become immortal he lived and lived,
lived and lived, lived and lived,
There where nobody died and died,
died and died, died and died,
And nothing could ever die because nothing
could ever live.
And nothing could ever live because nothing
could ever die.
There where nobody died and died,
died and died, died and died,
To become immortal he lived and lived,
lived and lived, lived and lived.
To become a mortal he died and lived,
died and lived, died and lived.
There once was a man who lived and died,
lived and died, lived and died.

Yes, the story is very short, but it is spoken in an ancient tongue, so there is no dust anywhere in these words. The mortal must learn how to die before he can learn how to live.

These words contain magic that will help you become truly mortal again, which is what you are so desperately trying to do.

Mortality is mortality, Chi, and immortality is immortality. Remember that the first is earned and the second is earned, but the second cannot be earned before the first is earned. Otherwise you risk turning that magic in upon yourself, and then it can only become dark.

And we immortals have another song:

198

*Do not forsake mortality for an assumed
immortal role,
Or Beng will certainly find you and come
to devour your soul.*

So, one day, Chi, when you have worked hard and have shown yourself to be worthy, when you have earned the right to be mortal, you may just be permitted a glimpse of the immortal Ancestral Homelands. For if you earn the right to be mortal, you will be on your way to earning immortality. And you will earn the right to see something of the Ancestral Caves, for by that time you will have learned to share a purpose with the spirit of water. By that time, you may finally understand what Life is really all about.

But we have a long way to go.

Remember, as Horki told you, it is all to do with the hard way, the courageous way, never the easy way. It is nothing to do with cutting corners.

Trust that I know all these forgotten ways, which to me are remembered ways. My advice may seem testing and rather blunt at times, but the curses of the old world are far worse.

But there is something else you need to know, Chi.

All those important ancestral spirits I speak of – Ravnos the sky, Kam the sun, Shon the moon, Puv the earth, Pahni the spirit of water, Yag the spirit of fire, Bavol the spirit of air, Chik the spirit of earth and of course many others – might just as easily deliver you a curse, should you not honour their laws.

Does that surprise you, Chi? You might even be shocked. You might believe that these spirits are all-loving, all-forgiving and always on your side, unconditionally, no matter what you do.

Not quite so.

Because for those mortals who abuse the Ancestral Homelands and turn their backs on Life, the penalty is harsh. Hear me, Chi, for I speak of those immortal spirits, including myself, who would love you and help you, those who would be your wisest teachers, those who would put themselves last in order to help you. But these same immortals would also teach you a good lesson were you to choose not to honour their natural laws.

That is the way it has always been. And that is the way it is destined to be.

So you will need to begin filling yourself with water now, no matter what it costs you, and you will need to let the water begin flowing in and out, in and out, trickling at first, but soon flowing smoothly and in a rhythm, like the tides of the great oceans of the world.

And if you do this, that water will flow directly out of the immortal world and into your mortal world, sustaining you.

Because if you never fill with water, how will you ever get to know what a reflection is all about? And how will Pahni ever be able to trust you? And if you do not know what a reflection is, or what water feels like, you are never going to know that you are there, present within your body.

What did I say about taking the time to look at yourself so that you know that you are really there?

Remember what I said: water cannot cause shadow.

I will tell Pahni I have told you all of this. I will pass the message on.

* * * * *

The ancient language I speak here, Chi, is strong and it is being stirred within you even as you are listening to me. This language is seeking to return you to Life, like the flame of a fire that is wishing to be rekindled. You will not have heard this language being spoken before in this way anywhere in the world, yet you may experience some faint and distant memory stirring within you when you hear it now.

Let water be your teacher and your guide where

learning this ancient language is concerned.

Once water has begun entering your soul again properly, you will start to hear what is really being said around you, especially in situations where previously you may have believed that nothing was being said at all. You will start to realise that this language has been spoken to you many times before. And you will recall mostly having heard it in the dead of night when you were being confronted with the obstacles that lay ahead on your path.

You need to know that this ancient language, Chi, is one which the Locollico spirits got to know very well in much earlier times. They learned to speak a specific dialect of it fluently. It may surprise you that they are able to speak the ancient and sacred language that all immortals know, and you may wonder why it has been permitted to happen. But remember the fish that taught the bird to breathe underwater, Chi. When lessons are not learned and Power takes their place, we lose sight of what is necessary and appropriate and real.

Remember that I speak the original language of all on earth, both mortal and immortal, the language of animals and birds and all the woodland and magical creatures that have ever existed. So while you are protected by understanding this language, you will also render yourself vulnerable to its strong magic if you do not take the trouble to understand it. For the One has never liked those who suddenly understand what he is saying.

The Locollico's ancient dialect goes like this:

> *Water in your soul*
> *Will never fill up that hole.*

And:

> *Never allow water to touch you*
> *In everything you do.*
> *Whoever you are, wherever you are,*
> *Water is not for you.*

It is a language that lives behind the scenes, behind your eyes, between your ears and within all those recesses that no one ever gets to talk about, Chi, those places I mentioned before, which people are rarely prepared to acknowledge.

But can you feel the meaning behind these words? Or do the words steal the meaning away?

This speech is not so much about words, or even rhymes, but about instilling fear. In your own Age of Hala you will have forgotten the earlier ways with words, for the very nature of Hala changes language beyond recognition.

You have a saying, Chi: 'I can feel it in my water.' And you need to feel all of this in your water at this time so that you are able to learn this ancient language all over again.

So there is a lot to learn, isn't there?

But know that although mortals no longer remember the old language, memory will begin to stir when courage is invited to step into a mortal's life. Courage is like a great spoon that reaches down into the depths of your inner being, Chi, stirring up all those things which the shadows lured you to believe about yourself.

Ruk was able to teach you a great deal about courage, because he also taught you about fear. And the Locollico will assist you in the preserving and cherishing of fear, hurt, pain, doubt, resentment and subservience – yes, preserving and cherishing these things, rather than understanding them.

The shadows will want to place their hands over yours as you take the handle of this great spoon I speak of and soon your hands and their hands will be stilled in an effort to silence the courage within you and to help you forget. Remember that stillness causes you to forget. Movement causes you to remember.

The Locollico do not want you to remember anything of the Old Land, Chi; they do not want to permit you even a glimpse. They just need you to recall what you believe you cannot do, and each time you do this you will have renewed your pacts with them once again.

The Locollico will be able to dress words in any way they wish. So the rhymes of the Locollico, like their cloaks, are all made of the same material, the same dust, which these spirits will be proud to demonstrate as they praise you for not being yourself. 'Ah, never mind,' they will say, with voices that nobody ever hears speaking and with lips that nobody ever sees moving. Their rhymes will drift about on the breezes of windless nights in their illusory world, a world constantly seeping into the vulnerable mortal world.

Yes, Chi, there is an ongoing battle between Bengesko memory, which binds you, and Devlesko memory, which bonds you, and where true freedom of the spirit is found. And this battle will rage as long as shadows continue to smother the earth.

You can encourage Devlesko memory, Chi, by believing that there was never a time when water was bad.

> *Water is good to feel.*
> *It keeps you alive and real.*

This is a Devlesko rhyme, Chi, sung by all the water spirits who serve Pahni, those who never harm her. And if you remember this rhyme, it will be difficult for Bengesko memory to cloud your vision.

So you must keep drinking in the water, drinking and drinking. But do not imagine that you should drink through your mouth. Do not think for one moment that I am implying consumption of many beakers of water. The water must be drunk through your soul. For your soul's thirst is ever stronger than your body's thirst. Yes, I am talking about emotion. And at the present moment there are many mortals dying of inner thirst, collapsing through lack of water, the thirst that is on the inside.

Remember that if you quench your soul's thirst, your body will no longer be as thirsty as it used to be. You may drink and drink and drink through your mouth. But a Locollico spirit will be observing you as you take yourself to your tap. 'How many beakers will you need?' he will ask.

And he will be happy to supply you with what he considers to be an appropriate amount so that he may keep your focus off your inner water. And he will refill and refill your beaker for you to ensure you are concentrating on your mouth and not on your soul. And I will be standing on the other side of you, removing that beaker every time he puts it in your hand. For it will be my intention to return the dark spell to its original home: the Shadow World, the world of illusion.

Because by putting your body where your soul should be, Chi, the Locollico are able to give you a different set of values regarding water, and this is not the way it should be. They are getting you to drink nothing but dust. Are you surprised that you are always so thirsty, always so dry on the inside?

The Locollico know that they must win the battle for your soul every single time the nature of your soul is questioned.

* * * * *

The River of Life has no beginning and no end, Chi. Do you remember hearing me say that? I repeat these words again now because I need to point out that a river's length bears no relation to its water.

The length and volume of a river can never be as meaningful as the quality of its water, just as the noise and length of your cry can never be as meaningful as what you are crying about.

There is a story about a man who drank a whole river, because he desperately needed to understand the River of Life. He sucked up every ripple, every wave, every last bit of foam and spray, until he grew very large, so large that he became a human river. But of course he was unable to make ripples, to make waves, to froth with foam and to shower spray. And why? Because the water contained within him developed volume. And the volume prevented the water from moving and all it could do was turn to dust. And the man became a dust river and is a dust river to this day as he shifts through the darkest regions of the Shadow Lands.

Remember that, Chi: water in volume prevents water in movement.

And whenever tears roll down your cheeks through sadness and your eyes smart through pain, fear or laughter, this is your soul's water. Whenever you feel moved beyond words, this is your soul's water. Whenever you feel cut up and hurt, this is your soul's water. It all flows into you, through you and out of you again with ease, just as Pahni moves her fast-flowing rivers, her trickling streams and her great waves with ease.

Mortals are able to drink and yet not drink, Chi. Most are trying to drink whole rivers. And they are therefore destined to become thirstier and thirstier as time goes by.

Ask yourself, can you make a boundary within water? Can you part it down the middle?

Of course you can't.

Dust is very different. Dust is malleable. It can be worked by shadows because within dust dividing lines and boundaries and joins and seams may easily occur where they do not need to occur. Should dust pile high enough and become congested enough, it can be moulded and shaped into anything one desires. Why do you think Ruk's hooded figure shifted when he moved, rather than walked? Dust shifts; water flows, bounces, bubbles, gurgles and sings.

Just allow the water to seep back into all the places inside you where dust may have collected up over the years, Chi. And do it now. Allow it to seep into your eyes and your ears, so that memory comes flooding back.

And here is a test for you, a test to know your water.

Stand somewhere where no one can hear you, open your mouth and then let out a cry. If you are measuring how long the cry lasts, you will know that you have very little water left within you.

Then you need to ask, is your cry meaningful at all?

205

Can you hear water in your voice, or mere dust? Do you believe your life is returning to you? Or are larger quantities of dust returning?

Remember that one who feels will see, but one who never feels will never know what lies beyond what is imagined.

I would also ask you: where is the dividing line that severed you from your ancestors? Who was it who made that cut so clean?

* * * * *

I have stopped pacing now. I am looking out of the cave towards a sunlit hillside. The landscape in the immortal world is as it has always been: natural, green, seasonal, comforting, sturdy and strong. It is simply being itself. And although I am still troubled by what is to come, I am calmed by the tranquil scene in front of me. I see the great mountains looming high, the tangled forests twisting away, the dipping valleys falling beyond, the vast plains stretching into the distance, the hot desert basking in mistiness.

I will go to see Pahni soon. I have no real news for her yet, but she will be pleased to hear that I am beginning to talk to you, Chi, that things are at last beginning to move.

And then I will stand beside the River of Life and think of you. I will think that our Boro Dikimangro is going to change things so much for you and for me.

You must go and find some water now, Chi. And you must look, and keep looking. And go beyond the water. Don't just look at your face. You know not to do that now. You know how important it is to look into your eyes, and through your eyes into your soul. And if you still cannot do that, think what the alternative will be: a shadow world crushing our beautiful mortal and immortal worlds, taking our memories away.

You must try to see yourself, Chi.

Will you take the time now to do that?

Perhaps you might want to do it for Horki and for Ruk, now that you have got to know them. Perhaps you might want to do it for others you don't yet know from your ancient past, others who would hold you just as dear.

Perhaps you might consider doing it for me now, Chi.

The Long Reflection awaits. I, Iuzio the Immortal, your most ancient grandfather, await. And the water is flowing just outside your door.

I am opening that door, Chi. I am standing on the bridge between our mortal and immortal worlds. I see more of you than you imagine, far more than you would ever believe.

And I am not going to let you go.

So you must trust in me now. Because though you still sometimes fade from me, drifting in and out of focus, sometimes rising up from the depths but not quite making it to the surface, I will wait. I will wait as I have always waited. Immortals have time on their side.

And even though you may not recall what I look like and may not be able to see me in great detail when you look into the water, know that I am there, somewhere within the ripples that keep forming, somewhere within the current that keeps rushing past, somewhere within the burst of dazzling sunlight that hits the water and momentarily blinds you.

Keep looking and you may just get a glimpse of my red hair and my blue eyes. You may just hear the faint stirrings of a familiar voice.

And who knows, you may just catch a glimpse of Ruk laughing or of Horki's kind smile.

Look for us all, Chi. Look for your family, and keep looking.

And hold on tight to my hand.

And now, Chi, in my ancient memory I will step out of my cave and walk to the river. And I will kneel down beside that river in the warm evening, just as I did many thousands of years ago when I first saw that dark cloud swirling, spiralling up behind me.

I will cup my hand and drink, as I used to do.

But this time, as I look out over the landscape, washed crimson with the dying sun, it will be different. For what is real will not be lost to us. The reflections will return to us again.

And I will walk away from that mortal place that is deep within my immortal memory and for the first time I will not look back and grieve for what was lost. I will openly celebrate what we are finding.

For though the battles of the human spirit will continue to rage, and though shadows will continue their fight to stop us from being who we are, and though there is still such a long way to go, Chi, we are about to remember.

Please contact the address below for programmes with Patrick Jasper Lee:

The Jal School of Arts and Life
PO Box 103
Hailsham
East Sussex
BN27 4HP
UK

www.jal-arts.com